the Richest
Kid in the
World

ROBERT HAWKS grew up in Michigan City, Indiana, and still thinks of it as home, despite moving about non-stop, including four years in England and many months in Turkey, Italy, and Germany. He now lives in Las Vegas with his wife Lynn, and his daughters Sarah and Valerie. Although he has yet to inherit sixty billion dollars, he does devote a portion of each day to planning what he'll do the second it happens.

the Richest Kid in the World

ROBERT HAWKS

AN AVON CAMELOT BOOK

THE RICHEST KID IN THE WORLD is an original publication of Avon
Books. This work has never before appeared in book form.

AVON BOOKS
A division of
The Hearst Corporation
1350 Avenue of the Americas
New York, New York 10019

Copyright © 1991 by Robert Hawks
Published by arrangement with the author
Library of Congress Catalog Card Number: 91-93006
ISBN: 0-380-76241-2
RL: 5.0

First Avon Camelot Printing: February 1992

CAMELOT TRADEMARK REG. U.S. PAT. OFF. AND IN OTHER COUNTRIES, MARCA
REGISTRADA, HECHO EN U.S.A.

Printed in the U.S.A.

OPM   10 9 8 7 6 5 4 3 2 1

For Sarah, and the Bear that
went wild.

Snagged

Monday was lousy. That was when I found out my best friend Carlos was moving to California. No warning, just hey, gotta go, sorry, man, goodbye.

Tuesday was lousy. It rained all afternoon, so we couldn't play softball in gym class, I failed a math test, and Carlos was still in California.

Wednesday and Thursday were also lousy. Wednesday I was late for school and Thursday I lost my lunch money somewhere outside Dalton's Pets, where a basset hound was howling in the window display for the fourth straight day. I walked by Carlos's house, where movers were finishing the packing up. I kept thinking about how Carlos had only just found out about the move. He'd barely even had time to tell me he was going. Standing there watching the men pack Carlos's bike into a box, I suddenly knew how the poor dog howling in the pet store window felt.

Friday looked like it was shaping up to be a *special* kind of lousy.

1

Amazingly so. First I got myself into a fight, and then got myself kidnapped, snagged by some guys in a helicopter. Talk about your truly memorable days . . .

I was dragging myself out to the vacant lot across the street from the school, getting ready for the fight—*beating,* really—which I brought upon myself at lunch, wondering what sort of scheme might get me out of it. Think quick, I was urging myself. Something has to happen, and fast.

Like what? The cavalry rushing to the rescue? Things from space? Comic book superheroes? The Royal Canadian Mounted Police?

Unlikely, I realized. Just as it was unlikely that I was going to be able to do anything in this stupid fight, other than maybe bleed at a few appropriate moments.

"Don't worry, Josh," said T.J. Bollin, who was walking beside me. T.J. was supposedly a friend; he sat behind me in Social Studies. T.J. said, "You're quick and smart. You can take him. And besides, even if you can't, he'll probably only hit you a couple of times."

I stared at T.J. in amazement. My friends *and* my enemies wanted to see the fight take place—for the entertainment value, I guess.

Some friends. Some enemies.

"Come on, clown," Lyle Walker was yelling, pushing us on our way to the midst of the gravel lot. "Come on and get what's coming to you."

Lyle was a legend.

Lyle was the King of the Ninth Grade.

2

Lyle was the guy always followed around by others, admired by kids who seemed to hang on his every word, but at the same time fear his every outburst. Lyle was the junior high guy elementary school kids all over the city were warned about.

Lyle had dark eyes, long, greasy black hair, and a voice that frightened cats and small dogs. At fourteen, he was two years older than I was, and at six feet at least a foot taller. At *least*. And although he was still trying to get a beard stubble to develop on his chin, Lyle dressed like a member of some outlaw motorcycle gang. He wore jeans and a denim jacket with a lot of patches, and he smoked when no adults were looking.

I presented a slightly less imposing figure. For one thing, I was only in the seventh grade, had shaggy blond hair, and dressed a bit more neatly. Actually, my clothes always looked as though they were right out of some mail-order catalog, which, of course, they were. I'd been living with Uncle Larry ever since my parents died, and he couldn't spare any time away from his get-rich-quick schemes to actually bother to shop in a store.

Memo to myself, number one twenty-two: Never let anyone pick out your clothes from a catalog while he's busy eating pizza and watching *Wheel of Fortune*.

Not that I cared about that sort of thing. If I had, I would have spoken up, said something. Clothes are not a big priority to me. My nose,

3

though, *is* important to me, and it was in immediate danger of being smashed. Lyle was grabbing me, pulling at my windbreaker. "I'm going to rip you up real good," he promised. "*Real* good."

Lyle didn't have to prove it; I was more than willing to take him at his word. Ripped up real good. Right, I sighed. That's the price I paid for being a quick wit in the cafeteria.

"When I get done with you," Lyle assured me, "you'll have to unlace your shoes just to see where you're walking."

There must be a law, I was thinking. There must be something written down somewhere which says that every junior high school in the world has to have a vacant gravel lot directly across the street, outside of school bounds, outside of the immediate authority of school officials, where fights and beatings may take place. And that law, I figured, must be routinely kept in place by ex-school bullies moved into positions of power and authority.

It was the only thing which made sense.

George Armstrong Custer Junior High School was behind us now, complete with its wooden plaque "To the Last Man," motto which Carlos and I had once covered with a piece of plywood so that it read, "Indians? What Indians?" But that was back in fun times, before Carlos left and before this new nonsense got rolling.

Prepare to be introduced to a pair of very unfriendly fists, I told myself. The thumping is about to begin.

4

What started all this, anyway? I tried to remember.

Oh, yeah. Lyle tripped some seventh grader at lunch, sending his food flying across the floor. Amidst the general laughter I was stupid enough to say to Lyle, "Why don't you pick on something your own size, or IQ? Like maybe a grapefruit?"

Oops. That was it. That remark really broke everybody up. Being the thug he was, Lyle reacted the way he always did: he challenged me to an after-school fight.

Definitely oops.

A lot of things could have prevented this fight—*beating*—from taking place. One, I could have brown bagged it that day. If I'd been packing jelly and tuna fish I would have already been seated, and been nowhere near the action scene by the cafeteria line. Or I could have eaten at Molly's Burgers. Carlos and I snuck off school grounds to go there sometimes. If I'd been at Molly's, enjoying sloppy french fries, then I wouldn't have been in the cafeteria. Carlos and I would have been swapping ball cards or something. Having fun.

Memo to myself, number six: What you don't see and don't know can't hurt you much. Once again the rule made sense. If I hadn't seen it, I wouldn't have known about the sad look on Carl Tulley's face as his feet were kicked out from under him. The fact that the guy's lunch went airborne wouldn't have bothered me.

Or, least likely of all, I could have just obeyed memo to myself, number one: In times of crisis,

5

keep your mouth shut. But I didn't; I couldn't. Guys like Lyle shouldn't always get things their way. So when Lyle tripped Carl Tulley, and then laughed as the poor kid stared out across the cafeteria floor at the smashed remains of his lunch, I stepped up and said what had to be said.

Maybe that was the problem, I reasoned. Maybe it was the grapefruit crack itself that was offensive. Maybe Lyle would have been less bothered by being compared to another fruit or vegetable.

Who was I kidding?

Standing in the lot, braced for pain, I looked at Lyle and cleared my throat, playing it cool. "Uh . . . Something wrong?"

Lyle smiled at me. Stepping eye to nose with me, blowing lousy breath, ready to punch, and then something happened.

Correction.

That was when *everything* happened.

Starting with a *whup-whup-whup* in the distance.

Huh? The *whup-whup-whup* increased to a heavy scream, quickly rising around us and drowning out all of the voices on the lot.

Then came the helicopter.

It dropped down out of the sky—it didn't actually *drop,* it did land properly—swooping in amidst a gale of wind and flying gravel raised by the rotor blades, but it arrived suddenly, without any warning. The noise exploded into a roar, and all activity on the lot came to a stop as everybody scattered to make way for this huge falling machine.

6

I thought it was crashing and ducked, raising a hand to shield my eyes from the stinging dust, wondering how big a chunk of metal was going to hit me when it exploded. Fortunately, though, it didn't slam down. It paused at the last second and landed quite nicely, quite easily. Dirt and dust were kicking and the chopper's engine roar drowned out everything, even Lyle's shouting. The sleek blue helicopter settled down on its skids less than fifteen feet away from us.

Red and blue lights flashed on the tail and underbelly. I saw then that the chopper bore the name GRIZZCO INTERNATIONAL. The doors bearing that name immediately flew open, and men jumped out.

Men in suits and mirrored sunglasses.

Men in suits and mirrored sunglasses with questionable attitudes about life.

The biggest man in a suit and mirrored sunglasses led the rest forward, towards where we were all standing. He was a huge bruiser, at least three hundred pounds, with a road map of white scars all over his face. He moved quickly and with urgency despite his size, as if he knew exactly where he was going and who he was going to beat up once he got there. I wondered how much extra fuel the chopper had to take on to carry this gorilla around.

Three other guys in suits followed, waddling like ducks in a row, and the kids standing around made room for them. The bruiser moved between me and Lyle. "Joshua T. Ellis?" he asked, giving

7

us both the once-over. "Which one of you is Joshua Ellis?"

I looked at the bruiser, over to the helicopter, then across at Lyle. None of which looked particularly inviting, so I pointed a finger at Lyle: "He is."

"*What?*" Lyle looked as if he might faint.

Fear. He *is* human, I thought.

The bruiser looked doubtful. He turned back to me and said, "We radioed ahead, and the word was Joshua Ellis was in the midst of an altercation across from the school."

"An alter-*what?*"

"Look, there ain't a lot of time here," said the bruiser. "Are you in fact Joshua?"

"Who *are* you guys?" I swallowed. "What happens if I say yes?"

"We get out of here. Fast. On that helicopter."

I looked at Lyle. Lyle still had plenty of fight—no, *beating*—left in him, and he was probably twice as intent on doing it now. I turned back to the big bruiser. "I guess I'm your boy."

The bruiser looked relieved. "Come with me, please."

"Sheesh," I said. "I guess if you insist . . ."

They did. As all the kids from the school watched, the four guys led me to the helicopter, its blades still rotating. I wasn't embarrassed. Better all those kids view my escape than my extermination. Actually, this was pretty cool, being taken away in a helicopter. And if this is a kidnapping, I thought, they're going to a lot of trouble to snag a kid with nobody to pay the ransom.

So I got in, and was no sooner inside the helicopter than it started its rise, leaving my stomach behind. The world dropped away even before the door was totally shut; it was as if the earth outside were in a plunge, but that wasn't the worst shock. Because I was stunned to see my Uncle Larry *there,* seated across the helicopter, but my surprise was maybe not as big as Uncle Larry's. He jumped a little bit. "Josh! What the—?"

I shrugged it all off, trying to be cool. Seeing my uncle there didn't make me feel any better. Uncle Larry was a used car salesman with a less-than-great reputation who spent half his time selling cars and the other half trying to avoid taking them back. "You can't cheat an honest man," he always said, but that never stopped him from trying.

I eased back in the seat, which was in a passenger compartment directly behind the pilot. Uncle Larry didn't change expression. His face was as tight as a raisin trying to come to a decision and he whispered, "Josh, I don't want you to panic, but we might be in some trouble."

I blinked. "What do you mean, trouble?"

"I mean (a) I don't know any of these guys, (b) they just dropped down onto the car lot and dragged me off just as I was about to make a sale, and (c) I think they have guns."

"Oh. So you mean *trouble* type trouble?"

"Yeah."

Terrific, I thought, watching my uncle squirm.

Larry finally made the big time, finally stepped on the wrong toes. Ordinarily I would have found amusement in that, but not now. Now I was thinking about what I wouldn't give to be back on the lot getting pounded by Lyle . . .

Grizzco

Uncle Larry looked glumly out of the window at the fields of green passing below. "We've cleared the lake," he announced. "Looks like we're leaving the state."

I watched the green checkered squares below where there used to be the blue of Lake Michigan. Then I closed my eyes. "We're in a lot of trouble," I said. "We're definitely in a lot of trouble."

We were arriving somewhere. The helicopter crossed in low over three long lines of chain link fences and wobbled as it raced across what seemed like an endless empty parking lot towards a huge factory complex of some kind. I saw that the GRIZZCO INTERNATIONAL logo was also painted in slanted blue letters across the sides of the building. The chopper breezed in at treetop level for the last five miles or so, giving my stomach lots of ups and downs.

Mostly downs.

The parking lot below us looked as if it could have held five thousand cars, but it was totally empty. "Where is everybody?" I asked as the chopper rocketed towards the building. "Slow work week?"

The bruiser shook his head. "Mr. Welsch's office gave all sixty-five hundred employees the day off, with pay. I guess he wants you two at the factory alone. No witnesses."

The bruiser smiled.

Uncle Larry looked confused. "Welsch? Do you mean *Grizzle* Welsch? The billionaire?"

The bruiser nodded. "Grizzle Welsch. The only man ever to be on the cover of *Time* magazine two weeks in a row."

"And he wants to see us?"

"Well . . . *See* might not be the right word for it."

Gulp.

There was another guy sitting in the helicopter with us, a sort of weasel of a guy who looked like an accountant. He reached forward and clipped a blue badge to my shirt. The badge had my photograph on it, a pretty goofy-looking photograph. "Hey," I asked. "Where'd you get my picture from?"

The accountant clipped a similar badge on Uncle Larry's plaid sport jacket and said, "Wear your badges at all times, and once we're on the ground, speak to no one until you're spoken to."

Uncle Larry, who was starting to regain his cockiness, said, "Or else what?"

"Or else," the bruiser hissed at Uncle Larry.

"Oh."

About half an hour of hovering passed, and the

helicopter eventually landed. A black car—a stretch limo, yet—rolled up just short of the chopper, and we were escorted over to it. The bruisers seemed very much on the alert for some kind of trouble. Next they drove us into a deep underground parking garage beneath the factory complex. Having never been in a limo before, I enjoyed the ride, but didn't get much of a chance to see anything before we were shepherded down a series of corridors and into a small conference room.

Wonderful. I couldn't *wait* to see what came next.

I looked around while we waited. One time, while I was in the sixth grade, I got caught making funny cartoon drawings of my teacher, Mrs. Mintzi. Obviously Mrs. Mintzi didn't appreciate my sense of humor; she got into a stuttering rage and sent me to the vice principal's office. Our vice principal, Mr. Krupal, was like most vice principals in the world—a maniac—and I had no intention of waiting around for the guy to recharge the batteries on his electronic torture devices. Instead, I snuck out the window and went home.

No such opportunity here. No windows. No air vents. No escape route of any kind. All that was in the room was a long wooden table with glass ashtrays and about fifteen chairs, although Uncle Larry and I were the only ones offered seats. The bruiser and the accountant remained standing behind us.

A few moments passed, and then the door clicked open. "Gentlemen," a voice announced.

"Mr. Grizzle Welsch." Uncle Larry stood along-side the bruiser and the accountant, and I did the same as the billionaire made his appearance.

The only problem was, the guy wasn't really there. Not *exactly*.

The great Grizzle Welsch made his entrance inside a television set, pushed on a heavy steel computer cart by a big bald guy in a dark suit. The big bald guy had grey eyebrows and skin like tanned leather. Instantly I thought of ball cards—no, better yet, *thug* cards, bully cards. Three in a pack: Lyle, the King of the Ninth Grade, Arnold Schwarzenegger, and *this* guy.

Yeah. I almost laughed. I pictured the big bald guy glaring out from a small photo on a piece of cardboard, smelling of brittle bubble gum. The reverse of the card, of course, wouldn't recount stolen bases or quarterback sacks but would be horrible statistics of violence and mayhem.

Right. Kids will buy millions. *Or else*.

The big bald guy wore a grey turtleneck sweater under a black suit jacket. He effortlessly guided the heavy cart through the doorway, and at the same time dismissed the bodyguards in a no-nonsense voice. "Thank you, Associates. Please stand dismissed."

They did; they were gone in an instant, closing the door behind them. Here we go, I thought, waiting for the other shoe to drop.

The big bald guy kept his place behind the cart, on which was a TV and some sort of compact disc player with a computer keyboard attached.

On the TV screen was an enormous face, in freeze frame.

"How do you do?" asked the man on the screen, jerking in sudden movement, as if he'd just been taken off "pause." "Greetings, of course," he said in a booming voice. "I apologize for the drama, but it was of some urgency that you both drop from public sight immediately."

"What's going on?" I asked.

"All in due time," answered the man on TV. "And there isn't much of *that* precious commodity."

The image on the TV screen froze again. The big bald guy typed something quickly on the keyboard and the man on the screen moved once more, speaking and saying, "We must move quickly to business."

That's the way it worked. We'd say something, but before the guy on the screen would respond, the big bald guy had to type something into the computer keyboard. Even Uncle Larry noticed it. "Hey, what's going on here?"

Good question, I thought, but I was also trying to figure out this feeling that I'd seen this guy on the TV somewhere before. What was it the bruiser had said? *Time* magazine? Yeah, that was probably it. I didn't read *Time* magazine, but I passed it on newsstands all the time. Memo to myself, number eleven: Any news you can't get off the headline isn't worth knowing.

"What's going on here?" asked Uncle Larry. "Is that . . . ?"

The big bald guy didn't speak, merely typed.

15

"Allow me to introduce myself," said the big face on the screen. "I am Grizzle Welsch. This is my assistant, Blackarc."

I asked the next question. "If he's Grizzle Welsch, why isn't he here? Why are we talking to a TV set?"

"Please excuse my physical absence," answered Grizzle Welsch, "but I'm rather indisposed at the moment and can't be with you personally. Unfortunately, I am dead."

The other shoe had dropped, and it was no sneaker, either. It was a big, heavy boot.

"Say *what?*"

Grizzle Welsch went on, explaining somewhat. "Fortunately, or unfortunately, my death was caused by a very lingering form of disease which we managed to keep in check, but not cure, for a very long period. This allowed me time to prepare. So although I could not gain immortality in spirit or form, I have managed—to a degree— to obtain that immortality in image, voice, and authority. I continue to speak, and my people— those closest to me, those I call my 'Associates'— continue to obey. Or at least I assume they do; otherwise you would not be hearing this message. And, as you are soon to find out, I can be a very, very stubborn man."

That shut us all up for a while. After all, what could we say to a dead guy?

The man on the screen smiled grimly. "Please. Make yourselves comfortable. We have much to discuss and exceptionally little time."

I cleared my throat. "Are you really dead?" The big guy typed again.

"Yes, I may have been dead for as long as a year."

"I don't understand. How can we be talking like this?"

"As I've indicated, I am a very stubborn man. I refuse to let death totally change my way of life."

"But *how?*"

Grizzle Welsch explained. "By taking advantage of CD and computer technology, I have tried to anticipate most of your questions and thoughts, and recorded my responses. We really are having a conversation; I am living beyond my death. Your input is typed into the keyboard, and the computer punches up the response I would have given, had I still been alive to communicate it."

"What is going on here?" Uncle Larry demanded again. He swirled around on his heels, apparently taking in the entire room. "I demand to know—"

Type, type, type.

"You should speak less and listen more," said the man on the screen. "You speak too much for a man who sells used cars and lives in a trailer court."

"*What?*"

"Yes. And it was in order to change both your lives that I had you rescued today."

This took Uncle Larry by surprise. "Rescued?"

"Please, could I speak for a few moments before

17

you say something foolish and annoy me? I think you'll be glad you listened."

Uncle Larry hesitated, but he didn't say anything.

I was still standing, and the face on the screen addressed me now. "Joshua. How are you today? Would you like anything? A cold drink, perhaps? Ice cream? A soda?"

I shook my head, confused. "No, thanks."

Type, type, type.

"Always polite," marvelled Grizzle.

"Do I know you?"

"Indeed you do," said Grizzle, chuckling.

"You didn't teach me math in the third grade, did you?"

"No."

I faked a look of relief. "That's good. I forgot to hand in some assignments, and I was worried this had something to do with my permanent record."

Hundreds of images flashed by on the screen in just a few seconds; all of them seemed to be me. Then the billionaire's face returned to the screen. "Joshua, do you remember—of course you wouldn't—a hot dog shared with an old man on a street corner?"

I thought about it. "Hey, wait a minute . . ."

"That was me. Yes."

I peered at the big man on the TV screen and finally recognized the face. "I remember that," I said. "You asked me to get you a hot dog off the cart because you didn't have any money, but then you got mustard and relish all over yourself. Sheesh, you were a slob."

"Well, you must pardon me. I hadn't eaten a hot dog off a pushcart in about twenty-five years."

I was amazed. "So you *were* rich. What did you need me to buy you a hot dog for?"

After the big guy typed, Grizzle shrugged. "I wanted to see if you really would do it. It was sort of a test of character."

I sat there in amazement.

"That shared lunch was more than just a meal," said Grizzle, starting on one of his annoying speeches—a habit of his, I was to learn—and he said, "For me that meal was a . . . a revelation. And a mission. You helped change my whole life that day there in the street, helped me rediscover that which I was."

"I don't understand."

"Yeah," said Uncle Larry. "Neither do I."

"Understand this, then: I, Anthony Thomas Martin Welsch—Grizzle to my friends—being of sound mind and deteriorating body, do hereby bequeath my entire fortune to young Joshua Ellis. My will and instruments of disposition dictate specific instructions that all of my wealth and holdings are to be placed in trust for Joshua immediately."

Uncle Larry looked as if the eyes might pop right out of his head. I just blinked. What was the guy talking about? He wanted to give me his money?

Uncle Larry looked like a dog who's just gotten

19

a heavy rubber bone dropped on his head. "That's crazy."

"Not at all. Just different. Is different always crazy?"

"No, but . . ."

Grizzle explained, "I have no living relatives. What better way to dispose of my resources than to locate some decent person to leave my money to?"

Good question.

"Legally, the estate shall lie in trust until Joshua's eighteenth birthday. Prior to that, an appointed executor, my assistant Blackarc, will manage and execute the holdings on his behalf. As of Joshua's eighteenth birthday, of course, he may do with the fortune as he wishes."

I'll admit it: my mind was blown. "Why are you doing this?"

Images of America flashed on the screen as the billionaire's voice continued. "I wanted to know if there were decent human beings left, or if it really was as they say on television. Are people really just cynical and selfish and mean these days? Or is there still reason to hope?"

I didn't know what to say.

Grizzle wrapped up his speech. "I realize this is all a bit of a shock, but a pleasant one, I hope. For whatever it is worth, I place myself and these recordings at your disposal. Blackarc will show you how to access the system, how to 'wake me up.' " Blackarc nodded; Grizzle continued to speak. "You will, of course, move into the house immediately. Arrangements to transfer Josh to his new school are already being made."

This threw me. "My *new* school? What's wrong with my old school?"

"It hardly meets the standards expected for the new billionaire director of Grizzco."

"Yeah, but if I'm going to be so rich, why bother with school at all?"

Blackarc answered that, with the first of what I eventually started calling his "fortune cookies" to me. He said, "An uneducated billionaire benefits no one but himself."

Again, I was confused. "So who else am I supposed to benefit?"

"It is our hope—Mr. Welsch's, as well as that of all the Associates—that you might be able to save the world."

I didn't hear that right. "Uh . . . Excuse me, did you say 'save the world'?"

"Yes."

I hated to be thinking like a computer, but that did not compute. "*Me?* Save the world?"

"Yes."

"Why me?"

Blackarc didn't shrug. He just said, "Someone should. Someone must."

"I couldn't even pass math. How can I save the world?"

Blackarc said firmly, "Apply yourself."

Groan. "Apply yourself," was something math teachers, school counselors, and vice principals said all the time. It never sounded good.

I have to admit my head was spinning, though.

This was like winning the lottery. No, it was bigger than the lottery. A lot bigger. This was like being told you'd never have to take another math test as long as you lived. Blackarc typed and Uncle Larry and Grizzle talked for a while, until finally I interrupted and asked, "Why? Why me?"

Grizzle answered. "You, young Joshua, are to be the instrument of my immortality. A computer system cannot run an empire, no matter how well programmed it is, so Blackarc and I shall teach you, educate you, raise you like a son."

"Uh . . ." I waved a finger. "This sounds a little flakey."

"I suppose it does. But what would you call having a conversation with a dead man?"

"More than a little flakey."

"Exactly."

Uncle Larry spoke, ignoring the weird talk to concentrate on the money. "Uh, how much cash are we talking about?"

"How much?"

"Yeah."

"In round numbers?"

"Yeah, sure."

"In round numbers . . . say, sixty billion dollars."

"Sixty billion dollars?"

"Yes."

Uncle Larry gulped. Hesitated a second. "That's a pretty round number."

"Yes, it is."

Uncle Larry gulped again, nodded, and was about to nod again when he changed his mind, I guess.

He fainted instead.

Three Acres

When people start giving their houses a name you know you're in trouble. That either means the house is haunted by horrible vampires and ghosts or the place is like a museum where all the furniture is covered in plastic and you're not supposed to touch anything. Neither would be a fun place to live. Three Acres was a little of both.

When I first heard the name I thought it sounded pretty neat. "Three acres of yard, that's pretty big," I said during the helicopter ride out. I tried to imagine it. "You could play football in a yard like that."

Blackarc was riding with us now, and he corrected me. " 'Three Acres' was named in honor of the original three acres owned by Mr. Welsch's mother, Miss Cassandra Dervish. Since that time there has been *significant* expansion."

I was about to learn what Blackarc's idea of *significant* was.

As we flew out, I tried to get used to everything that was happening to me. It wasn't easy, but at least all the new faces around us were starting to have names. For example, the big bruiser with the scars who came to get me at school was Mr. Feldman, a Grizzle Welsch Associate and now my "personal security representative."

"What's that?" I asked.

"Bodyguard," he answered. He was up front, sitting beside the pilot in the copilot's seat, and he didn't look back when he answered.

"Cool," I said, wondering what Carlos would think to see me whizzing around in a private chopper with a 'personal security representative.' Wait a minute, I thought, forget Carlos a second—what would *Lyle,* King of the Ninth Grade, think when he found out I had a bodyguard? I tapped Feldman on the shoulder. "Hey," I said, "could you beat somebody up for me?"

Feldman nodded, took a notepad and pen from his suit jacket pocket, and said, "I'll need the 'somebody's' name, and how badly you want him hurt."

"For sure. It's—"

I cut myself off. Blackarc was staring right at me. I expected him to jump up and say hey, you can't have your personal security representative go down to the junior high and just beat up anybody you want. Only he didn't, and I could have, I guess. I had the power. Feldman was going to do whatever I wanted him to, and he wasn't even going to ask why.

"Hey," I said, "Don't you even want to know why I want the guy beat up?"

Feldman shrugged. "That's not really my business. I just do what the boss tells me."

"And I'm the boss?"

"You're the boss."

Power. I could order Lyle thrashed to within an inch of his life and not give it another thought. Or I could just blow the whole idea off and forget about poor Lyle. I had power, but did that mean I had to use it?

Blackarc sat there quietly, as if he were waiting for me to make up my mind. The guy was starting to make me nervous.

What would Uncle Larry do, I wondered? That took a full second to figure out—he'd do it in a heartbeat. He'd have Feldman beat up Lyle in a second.

But did that mean I had to?

No, I thought, backing off. "Never mind," I told Feldman. "It's not that big a deal."

Which turned out later to be a mistake, by the way. A big mistake. I should have sent Feldman after the King of the Ninth Grade when I had a chance. I should have had him rip Lyle's lungs out. But I didn't, and that's what's important.

Blackarc didn't react to my change of mind, either. If I'd expected him to give me a big hug and call me a hero or something I was way off. He just stared straight ahead.

Anyway. The helicopter pilot's name was Mike— "Mike Mince," he said, never taking his eyes from the view ahead. I switched places with Feldman and rode up front with Mike the pilot, and he started to do some tricks with the stick. He rocked the chopper back and forth, taking us up a few thousand feet. Then, pointing the stick forward, he made us race towards the ground until he pulled up, just skimming the tops of the trees with the landing skids.

"Hey," yelled Uncle Larry. "What is this, astronaut training?" He was starting to turn green, but I loved it. I looked over at Mike the pilot and asked, "Can I try?"

"Sure," said Mike the pilot. "Take hold of the copilot's stick."

It was just in front of me and I grabbed it with both hands.

Mike still had hold of his, though; I mean, he didn't just shrug and say "Take over, kid"—he wasn't a complete idiot. He explained the controls to me, pointing out the altimeter gauge, which showed how high we were, and the airspeed indicator, which showed how fast we were going. We were at eighty-five hundred feet, doing two hundred and twenty-five miles an hour.

This caught me by surprise. "Two hundred and twenty-five miles an hour!" I yelled. "That's the fastest I've ever gone in anything in my life! Even Uncle Larry doesn't drive that fast. Sheesh, I hope we don't hit anything."

"It's best not to hit anything if you're doing *twenty-five* miles an hour," said Mike the pilot. Next he pointed out the LFI—Level Flight Indicator—which was a gauge with a little airplane on it. "That tells whether you're flying straight and level, or whether you're going up, down, or turning. Next to it is the compass which shows our heading, the direction we're flying in."

I nodded. "Yeah, yeah, I got it. How do I fly?"

"Hold your horses," he said. "The stick controls the blade overhead; when you move it, the blade pitches right, left, forwards, or backwards."

"What about the foot pedals?"

Mike shook his head. "Those control the stabilizer—that's the blade on the back. Better let me handle that one for now. Go ahead and take the stick."

I did. "Can I move it?"

Mike nodded. "Go for it, kid."

I went for it, and it was great. When I moved the stick, the chopper reacted immediately. Enough to give a person the willies, anyway. Once I pulled it too far back and Mike had to jump in and grab the stick just to keep us from crashing, I guess. "Steady," he said. "Helicopters can't do loops."

"Sorry."

Meanwhile, Uncle Larry was changing colors like a cartoon lizard. Even Feldman the bodyguard didn't look so hot. I looked back at both of them and laughed. "Isn't this great?"

Only Blackarc looked unimpressed. He looked the same no matter what happened. The guy was *definitely* starting to make me nervous.

Mike the pilot took over again and flew on. About five minutes later, he spoke over his shoulder. "Coming up on Three Acres now, Mr. Blackarc."

I stared ahead, looking for the place. All I could see was a small village surrounded by rows and rows of trees. "Where is it? Is it close to that town?"

"That's no town. That's the Three Acres estate."

Yet another gulp.

Three Acres the estate consisted of about seven buildings, a golf course, pools, tennis courts, and other such nonsense. The place was surrounded by a mile and a half of apple orchard, the leaves of which were all changing color now, since it was October. It seemed as though every possible shade of orange and red were down there, along with a few that didn't seem possible. "That's the yard?" I asked.

"Yeah, the front yard anyway," answered Mike the pilot, bringing us down lower.

"I'm glad I'm not the one who has to rake up the leaves."

The helicopter swung over it all and behind the big house, towards where there were three big red circles on the pavement, just beyond the tennis courts. The landing pads. There was already another helicopter sitting on one of them; it looked just like the one we were riding in, bearing the words GRIZZCO INTERNATIONAL. Our chopper settled down beside it, and Mike the pilot threw a bunch of switches on the chopper dashboard, shutting down the engine.

Uncle Larry still looked like he was made out of Jell-O. I figured I'd have to help him out of the helicopter and I said, "Hey, you all right?"

That woke Uncle Larry up. "No! No, I'm not all right! I'm sick, I'm tired, and I'm lucky to be alive!"

"Cheer up," I said, looking out at the buildings and grounds. "I think this is going to beat the

28

Highway 217 Trailer Court." The trailer court was where we lived—prior to that afternoon, anyway.

Uncle Larry came to his senses then, and we both climbed out of the helicopter. His eyes went wide as he looked around; then he hesitated and grabbed me by the arm. "Josh, wait a minute. Listen."

"Yeah?"

Uncle Larry leaned in and whispered to me. "This could be like in those movies. You know, the ones where the guy sells his soul to the devil to get rich and powerful?"

I thought about it. "Yeah."

"So remember: if anybody asks you to sign away your soul in return for all this money and stuff—do it."

"Right."

Ahead of us, Blackarc pointed out a pair of nearby golf carts. "Let's go."

"Can I drive?" I asked. I explained that I knew how to drive a golf cart, since it wasn't a real car or anything and couldn't be much more difficult to operate than a go-cart. Carlos had two go-carts and we used to drive them all the time.

None of which impressed Blackarc, or Uncle Larry. Feldman the bodyguard drove one, with Uncle Larry, and I rode with Blackarc in the second. We left Mike the pilot back with his helicopter.

"So what's next?" I asked Blackarc. At first I didn't think he was going to answer, because he seemed to be brooding, but then he said, "Three

Acres consists of several different buildings and facilities, as well as staff housing. Many of the staff have their husbands, wives, and children on the grounds with them; Mr. Welsch always encouraged this. He considered—*considers*—them to be his family."

"So why didn't he leave the money to them?"

Blackarc shrugged. "Perhaps he did. Perhaps he only left you in charge of it."

"I thought you were in charge."

Blackarc tightened his lips. I guess I hit a nerve. "It's time for you to greet the staff," he said.

Our golf carts were rolling up a long driveway now; ahead lay the big house. It looked like something the president or a king might live in. Or a rich Hollywood movie star. Or, I thought with a sudden giggle, me. "Can I ask a question?"

"Absolutely."

"Why did everybody call him Grizzle? Grizzle Welsch, I mean."

Blackarc seemed uncomfortable for a moment. "I believe he preferred to be called Grizzle. I'm not quite sure—"

"You never did."

"What?"

"I've never heard *you* call him that. It's always 'Mr. Welsch' to you. And he's dead now, so what difference does it make?"

"Yes. Well . . . familiarity breeds contempt."

"Oh. So you didn't want to get too close to him?"

"Or something."

Next we went inside the house and met the staff.

"This is the Great Hall," Blackarc explained as we entered. No doubt, I thought. The room was so big and quiet it felt as though we were sneaking into a church. It *was* a lot like a church. First off, the place was crowded with people, grownups and children, all of them watching the four of us as we entered and walked first to a staircase, and then climbed to a balcony which overlooked everything. I felt nervous because it seemed like all those faces were staring up, watching me.

Waiting.

Waiting for what?

Blackarc startled me. "So what do you think?"

I shrugged. "Uh . . . it's a great hall, I guess. But I wouldn't know what a not-so-great hall looks like. What am I supposed to think?"

Blackarc nodded, as if I'd just said something really important. He looked at Uncle Larry then, and asked him his opinion. Uncle Larry stuffed his hands in his pockets and shook his head, whistling. "I'll bet this place set the old man back a bundle. What's a setup like this run, anyway? Before utilities, I mean? I'll bet your electric bill is just out of sight . . ."

Blackarc just looked disgusted. He was starting to do that a lot, too. I don't think he was too impressed with Uncle Larry.

Blackarc addressed all the people below us then, introducing us. "As you all know," he said, "Mr. Welsch's—*Grizzle's*—instructions were very

31

specific. A boy would be assuming complete control of Grizzco, Three Acres, and Welsch Industries. We've always known that. We've just never known who. Well, I will now introduce you to that boy: Master Joshua Ellis . . ."

There was applause now, but not a lot of it. Just a sort of "hello" applause; it wasn't like I'd just shot a winning basket or hit a home run or anything.

Blackarc nodded at the crowd and whispered to me. "You are expected to say a few words."

That startled me. "Huh?"

"Speak to the crowd," he said.

"Say *what?*"

"Say 'hello.' "

I was beginning to realize Blackarc wasn't exactly happy about all of this.

I looked down at all the people down there, especially the kids. There were even some my age. The only other time I'd ever been up in front of that many people was when I was in the all-school Halloween play two years ago. The play was *Night of the Lizard Who Delivered Pizza* and Carlos and I played zombies. All we had to do was stand there in front of all those people and look terrified. We were both great.

My pizza delivery boy zombie routine wasn't going to work with this group, though. They were down there waiting for me, and I realized it was pointless. No matter what I said, it was going to come out stupid and make me look as though I just fell out of a tree on top of my head.

So I shrugged. "Hi," I said. "How's it going? I guess I'm the new kid on the block."

For some reason *that* impressed them. Laughter broke out and so did the applause; this time it was more real, louder. I felt a little more confident. "I have no idea what I'm doing here," I said. "I feel like that kid in that horror movie— everybody in the world knew who he was. Everybody but him."

More applause. I was doing good.

Of course it was *easy* to do good with this crowd. No matter what I said, they applauded. I could have yelled out, 'Blackarc is a cheesehead!' and they would have clapped their hands off. It was as if I were king, as if they were under strict orders to make me feel like royalty.

Why? *Was* I royalty?

Grizzle (the computer Grizzle, anyway) and Blackarc said I was rich. Did being rich make you a king or something? Ruler of all you surveyed? Did money do this to people?

I looked down at the crowd. They were still there, and I was definitely out of things to say. What did they want? A blessing? A raise?

That was when I saw Miss Lisa.

I didn't know that's who she was then, of course. All I knew was that there was a girl my age staring a hole right through me, and she was the only one down there not grinning like a maniac. She had blond hair tied back in a ponytail, and she was looking up at me as if I'd just said something terrible to her dog. Something terrible like, "What's the matter, you never been

33

run over by a car before?" She looked as though she wanted nothing more than to stuff me in a sack, fill the sack with rocks, and push it off a bridge.

I liked her as soon as I saw her.

The Not-so-haunted House

There's a lot to tell about Three Acres, but the real important thing, I guess, is the fact that it was almost, sort of, but not quite, haunted. This isn't easy to explain.

They gave me my own room right after the big scene in the Great Hall, and I didn't have time right then to wonder any more about the girl who hated me. Blackarc and Feldman the bodyguard turned me over to Norman, a short skinny guy with a red bow tie and a brown mustache.

Terrific, I thought. Norman looked like Pee Wee Herman with fur on his face, and he was taking me to what he said was my room. It was three floors up, though, and first we had to ride an elevator. Not just any old elevator, though, as I was about to learn. The doors opened, we walked on and a high-pitched voice said, "Kindly call out your floors, please."

"What?" I looked around the elevator, thinking Norman had just tried to impersonate a parrot.

"Kindly call out your floors, please," said the voice again.

"How'd you do that?" I asked, looking around. "Your lips didn't even move."

"The elevator—the whole house—is computer assisted," explained Norman. He said that as though he were talking to some kid or something. Which I guess he was.

The elevator tried again. "Kindly—"

"Penthouse," said Norman, irritated.

"Thank you," said the elevator. The doors closed, and the elevator started to rise, saying to us, "Have a *nice* day."

I shook my head, amazed. "A talking elevator? That's pretty neat. Who thought of that?"

Norman frowned. "Stupid thing makes me crazy. I usually take the stairs."

"Stairs?" said the elevator then. It sounded insulted. "You call what we have in this place stairs?"

I looked at Norman and started to say something, but he just shook his head and raised a finger to his lips, telling me to be quiet.

The elevator rattled on all the way up, bad-mouthing the stairs. "Stairs, you call them? Death traps, if you ask me. Do you know how many people break their necks every year falling down stairs in their own homes?"

"No," I said. "How many?"

Mistake. Norman glared at me. I found out why: the elevator didn't know, and I—this is loony, I know—had *embarrassed* the stupid thing. "Well . . ." it stuttered, "quite a lot, I'm sure. More than a few."

"Uh huh."

36

"And the basements," it added. "What about the basements?"

"What *about* the basements?"

The elevator sounded smug. "The stairs don't go down there, do they, now? That says something for the safety, quiet, and efficiency of a good elevator over tramping up and down a dangerous flight of stairs, thank you very much."

I looked at Norman. "What's it talking about?"

"Who knows?" said Norman. "For some reason the elevator is convinced this house has two basements."

"It *does*," said the elevator very strongly. "A basement and a *sub*basement."

"Oh, yeah?" asked Norman. "Then how come nobody ever gets to see it?"

"Because you're not supposed to see it. That's why the stairs don't go down that far. That's why only the elevator goes down there."

"Okay, so take us down to see it."

"No."

"Why not?"

"Because Grizzle said to hide it."

"Why would Grizzle tell you to hide a basement?"

"Maybe for the same reason he made you head of his household, *Normie*. Maybe he just got stupid one day."

"Hey, hey, *hey*," I said, looking at Norman *and* the elevator. "Take it easy, come on." I couldn't believe what I was hearing: a guy was having an argument with a talking elevator. And *losing*.

"He started it," said the elevator.

"Did not."

"Did so."

"Guys . . ." I said.

"Penthouse," announced the elevator, doors opening.

"Come on . . ." said Norman, jumping out very fast. I followed, just as Norman stuck his tongue out at the elevator. The machine saw it with its electric eye, blew back a raspberry and slammed its doors shut.

Crazy. This was crazy.

"Is this whole house like this?" I asked.

"Not the stairs," said Norman, still steamed over the elevator ride. "The stairs are very polite."

(They were, too, as I found out later. The stairs liked to talk baseball. The stairs, I found out, were Cubs fans.)

Anyway . . . We were in a hallway now, but it was a small one; we were also standing in front of these big double doors, which Norman pushed in. "This is to be your room," he announced.

Room? My head was spinning. This place was *incredible*. It looked more like a big apartment than a room—an apartment you could land an airplane in.

"My room?" I said, shaking my head. "This is bigger than our whole trailer."

Norman twitched his nose. Perched above his mustache, his nose looked like a rabbit chewing on brown grass. Obviously he wasn't impressed that Uncle Larry and I lived—or used to live—in a house trailer.

"It's not so bad," I assured him. "Oh, they rock

38

a bit during thunderstorms, what with the rain and the wind beating on them, but Uncle Larry and I just pretend we're pirates crossing the ocean during a bad storm."

The rabbit was still eating. "Pirates?"

"Yeah. Uncle Larry stands on the big chair and screams out orders. You know, 'Batten down the hatches! Batten them down!' That means I need to make sure the windows are all closed."

"Windows. Closed. Of course."

I was really getting into the story now, remembering the last time it had happened, Uncle Larry and I caught in this big storm. "We're rocking back and forth in the trailer, just like on a boat. I'm battening the old hatches, and Uncle Larry stays at the wheel, keeping us set on course no matter what. Plus, he empties the buckets in the living room. Under the leaks, I mean."

"Buckets. Yes."

"Well, not exactly *buckets*," I said. "Mostly we use pots and pans. From the kitchen cupboard. Of course it's not really a kitchen . . ."

"I get the point," said Norman, cutting me off. "I am *supposed* to show you your room." He said the word *supposed* as though he was going to be shot by a firing squad if he didn't get on with it, so I shut up.

He showed me the room. Rooms, really. Three and a half, I guess. I had my own bathroom, with a tub big enough to float a shark in, plus a room to sleep in. That alone was actually a room and a half, though, because the other end was set up with a couple of dressers, a desk, and two chairs. There was a big screen TV with a VCR connected, bookshelves full of books, a big stereo (eleven speakers around the room—I counted) and a computer screen and keyboard. I checked the closet to see if there was a car parked inside. There wasn't, but it was big enough.

No way could this be the room of a kid. "Who used to live here?" I asked.

"This was Griz—" Norman cut himself off, and I realized he wasn't mean, just upset. "This was Mister Welsch's room," he explained. "No one has occupied it since."

"Wow," I said, immediately wondering whether the room was haunted. I thought about the elevator and asked, "Does the room talk?"

"Not to me," said Norman. He walked over and opened the curtains. "At least never to my face. I have no idea of what it might be saying behind my back."

"You worry about what the rooms say about you after you leave?" I shook my head. "Is this a crazy house, or what?"

"Could be. Are you crazy?"

I thought about it. "I don't think so. Anyway, I don't feel crazy. Two plus two is four, right?"

He thought a second. "Yes."

With a shrug I said, "I guess I'm okay, then. They say the first thing to go is your ability to do simple math."

"Who says that?"

"I don't know. Math teachers, I think."

Norman nodded. "Very good, sir."

"Is it? Really?"

"No. But it's the sort of thing I'm expected to say to you when I don't have the slightest idea what you're talking about."

I had to laugh. (Well, I didn't *have* to, but I wanted to.) I was starting to like the guy, attitude problem and all. He left and I wandered around the penthouse, going through the drawers and looking under the bed and stuff. I looked at some of the books on the shelf—nothing *I'd* ever want to read, that was for sure—and I clicked the TV on and off with the remote control. The room had cable, but no tapes for the VCR. I tossed the remote control onto the bed and looked at the computer. Just for the heck of it I reached out and tapped the keyboard.

"Hello."

I jumped. It was Grizzle Welsch. His picture appeared on the TV screen and his voice surrounded me. The dead guy was talking to me *in stereo*.

"Sheesh . . ." I said, backing away from the computer.

"How do you like your room?" asked Grizzle. There was a slight smile on his face.

I didn't know how to answer. Back at the Grizzco office, Blackarc had typed all of our replies; now I didn't know what to do. I can't type—I can hardly write, my handwriting's so bad. But Grizzle told me I didn't have to worry about that. "Here at Three Acres we have voice interaction. Just speak aloud, and the information will be processed by the computer main-frame, and I'll be able to answer."

"What?" I said. "Just talk anywhere? Like in the elevator? Just start talking and you'll answer?"

"No. That would be too confusing; the auto-talk system only works at certain terminals. Here, in the den, and in the subbasement."

Subbasement. "Oh, so the elevator was right, huh? This place does have two basements."

"Yes. The subbasement is where they keep me."

"You mean—"

"No, Josh, not my body. I'm talking about me, the computer. The basement is where all the working parts are."

"Oh. I hope your basement doesn't flood like Carlos's basement used to."

"It doesn't."

"A basement under a basement. Pretty neat," I said.

"Yes . . ." said Grizzle-the-computer slowly, like he was thinking about something. "But I think it might be best if you kept that to yourself for now. Otherwise we'll have no place to work together privately."

"Right," I agreed. "Sort of like a Batcave. Or Superman's Fortress of Solitude. Or Ratman's Sanctuary." I started going on about it. "Did you ever read the Ratman comic books? He's absolutely the coolest ever. He's like super cool, you know what I mean? Ratman is like—"

"I get the point," said Grizzle, waiting for me to shut up. As time went on, I found out that was part of the computer program: whenever I would start to babble on about something the computer couldn't make heads or tails out of, Grizzle would just cut me off by saying, "I get the point."

"Okay," I said. "So what was the deal with that elevator?"

Grizzle chuckled. "Three Acres is a grand experiment in technology, computer assists, and such. Certain of the inner systems are . . . uh . . ."

"The elevator's a nerd, Grizzle."

"Nerd." Grizzle seemed to think about it, then laughed. "Yes, some of the personalities did come out a bit questionable."

I sat back on the bed then, and asked, "Are you really dead?"

"Yes." He said it with no emotion.

I shook my head. "This is so weird. I mean, this house is haunted. The elevators and stairs talk, your ghost is floating around inside a computer, and God only knows what's next . . ."

"What's next is this. You and your uncle will freshen up—that means take a shower, by the way—and then you will eat a good dinner and go to bed early. Tomorrow, as you know, is Saturday, and there is no school. You do, however, have a press conference scheduled, and you must be well rested and prepared."

"A *press conference*?" This made me sit up again.

"Yes. Blackarc will brief you."

"Blackarc, huh? Listen, I don't know about this guy Blackarc—"

43

"Blackarc is one of my most valued Associates."

I remembered Blackarc talking about Grizzle. I didn't think Blackarc could like anyone. "I've known Blackarc for years. I would trust him with my life."

"Yeah, that's easy for you to say. You're dead."

"Tomorrow's your first day as a billionaire, Josh. You'll need all the help you can get."

I nodded. "Right."

Grizzle didn't say anything else right then. Maybe his batteries were running low.

Norman came back up a few minutes later with clothes for me. *My* clothes, the ones I'd left hanging in my closet that morning. "As we had no idea what you might want, we didn't buy new clothing for you, so a company chopper was dispatched to your house trailer." Norman obviously wasn't too happy with the contents of the suitcase he was lugging in.

"Wow," I said. "You guys brought all my clothes from the trailer?"

"No. We brought the trailer."

"Huh?"

"Your uncle's trailer was lifted by the chopper and brought to the south lawn."

"Wow. I bet Mr. Warner was surprised. He's the trailer court manager."

Norman smiled a totally phony smile. "How nice."

I laughed again. Norman was so unfunny he *was* funny. I took my shower and got dressed, following him down to the stairs. This was where

I first talked to them. On the way I asked Norman, "How much do you get paid to do this?"

"Not enough to do this," he said.

We went to dinner.

The Worst Man in the World

Dinner was weird, at least to me, a kid used to eating cereal over the sink. We ate in a huge dining room and sat at a huge table. I asked if the dining room talked, and they all looked at me like I was crazy. When I say "they" I mean Uncle Larry, Blackarc, and our guests. The first was a very tall, businesslike woman named Andy, short, she said, for Andrea Charlene Hampton Everett Morse.

"How come you have so many names?" I asked. She didn't get a chance to answer that, because next Blackarc introduced the other guest, the blond girl who'd hated me on sight in the Great Hall. Blackarc called her Miss Lisa. She was Andy's daughter.

"Hey," I said. "You know this house has rooms and elevators and stairs that talk to you, just like they were human or something? The staircase and the elevators *hate* each other . . ."

I stopped talking because the great Miss Lisa didn't look as though she were going to say anything either.

As we ate, I peeked at Miss Lisa and caught her peeking at me, for whatever that's worth. She still didn't look happy. I wasn't happy either. The food was way too fancy. I'd have killed for a slice of pizza.

Memo to myself, number seventeen-A: Never eat anything that takes more than six ingredients to make. After the salad they brought out something they called a quiche, and I almost gagged on the first bite. It tasted like soggy cat litter mixed with mayonnaise. "Don't you guys have any hamburger? I'd love a hamburger." The guy serving the food looked as though I'd just slapped him. "I eat hamburger almost every night. Uncle Larry doesn't like to cook much."

"I don't like to cook *at all*," laughed Uncle Larry. He didn't seem to be having any trouble with his food; he spoke with his mouth full, elbowing Andy as he talked. "We used to live on TV dinners and microwave food, you know? But Josh is learning to do crazy things with a pound of hamburger. Eggs, too. Josh can boil an egg with the best of them."

"Yes. I can imagine," said Andy. She had a nose twitch that reminded me of Norman's sneer.

Hold it, I thought. Nobody questions Uncle Larry's purpose in life more than me, but for some reason it really bothered me to watch Blackarc, Andy, and Miss Lisa all sitting there looking so superior just because they could choke down a dinner that would make a billy goat sick.

Andy was my lawyer, Blackarc said. When I asked why I needed a lawyer he said, "Andy is a

47

longtime Associate, and we've picked her as your attorney to represent you in any legal proceedings that might become necessary, as well as accompany us to tomorrow's press conference."

Andy frowned at me, saying, "I'm going to proceed with any necessary litigation and, shall we say, forestall any unnecessary complications."

"Say *what?*"

That was the only problem with Andrea Charlene Hampton Everett Morse. She was a nice enough lady, but she did not speak English as we know it. Blackarc had to keep translating.

Blackarc cleared his throat. "She'll go to court, if we have to, and bash the other guys' brains in."

"What? You mean fight?"

"Yes, but with books, not baseball bats."

I nodded. "Okay. But why am I going to need help? Is something wrong?"

Andy put a briefcase on the table next to her. "Nothing is terribly amiss. Things are just... well, *complicated*. First of all, of course, is the matter of the code key."

"Code key? What are you talking about?"

She opened the briefcase and pulled out a chain. There was a funny-looking blue key hanging from it, and she passed it across to me. "Maintain this on your person at all times."

I looked at Blackarc. "Wear it around your neck," he said.

"Why?" I asked. The key looked a little dorky to me, if you'll excuse the expression. "What's it for?"

"Grizzco is a big corporation, with numerous valuable assets and holdings."

"Huh?"

Blackarc translated: "Lots of money and stuff."

"Oh."

"As many of our orders and transactions are conducted via electronic transmission, we have to know for sure that the person giving the orders is—well, is who he or she is claiming to be. Otherwise an imposter could swiftly plunge the corporation into total chaos."

I looked at Blackarc. He said, "We need to know who we're talking to on the phone, or else we might do something stupid."

"Oh."

Andy started to speak, but she stopped herself and said to Blackarc, "Tell him how it works."

Blackarc nodded and said to me, "The way it works is this: whenever you need to give an order or get some secret information from the computer system, stick your key in the lock. That way the system—everybody—will know it's you."

"You mean like the computer ID on *Star Trek?*"

"Sort of, yes."

I checked out the key again and thought about it. "I didn't need any ID to talk to the computer in my room."

"That's true, but all you can do is talk. To give orders to the computer, you have to use one of the two main station computers. There's one here in the study, and one at the Grizzco office; we'll show you that one tomorrow. But don't lose the key. That's the only one in the world; Grizzle left it just for you to wear. If anyone else got hold of it, the computer wouldn't know that. It would think the orders were coming from you."

"Orders like what?"

Miss Lisa surprised me—and everybody—by speaking up then. "Orders like sell Three Acres, fire everybody, mess up all our lives."

"Huh?"

"That's what they want to do, isn't it?" asked Miss Lisa. Her anger was flowing over, and it wasn't all aimed right at me. "Close up Three Acres, fire everybody, ruin everything Grizzle tried to start?"

Uncle Larry was slowly catching the drift, and he didn't like what he was hearing. "You mean somebody might contest this whole thing? Try to say Josh shouldn't get the money?"

"We're allowing for every possibility."

Oh yeah? I wondered. *Every* possibility, huh? What if somebody just decided to kill me? Then I remembered Feldman, the bodyguard, and I swallowed hard. Maybe Blackarc *was* considering every possibility.

Andy tried to explain. "Even before Grizzle's death, there were problems within the corporation. Certain elements, certain *factions* wish to gain control of the company. These factions have designs on *complete* control. These factions have not been altogether pleased with Grizzle's plan of operations . . ."

I looked at Blackarc. "Factions?"

"There's a guy who wants to take over, change the way we've been doing things."

"One guy?"

"Yes. A very special guy named Kurt Falco."

"Special? What's so special about him?"

Blackarc didn't blink. He said, "Kurt Falco is the worst man in the world . . ."

I got to meet the worst man in the world the very next morning.

Because the next day, I had to go to the press conference to let the world know I wasn't Josh Ellis, twerp kid anymore. Now I was Josh Ellis, twerp billionaire.

We took the chopper back to the Grizzco factory; Andy came along, but not Miss Lisa. The highlight of the flight was Mike the pilot's letting me work the stick again. I was starting to get better; he even said so. "How old do you have to be to take flying lessons?" I asked.

Mike the pilot grinned at me. He reached over and snapped down a switch. "You really want to learn?"

"Yeah, this is great."

Uncle Larry didn't think so, of course. He was in the back changing colors again. I have to admit I was mean—I took it as a challenge to make him sick. But no matter how I rocked the helicopter, I couldn't get him to throw up. Uncle Larry's tougher than he looks.

Mike the pilot took over again when we got close to the factory, and brought us down for another limo ride to the parking garage. This time I asked the driver of the car what his name was. I figured if I was going to be boss I should get to know everybody. He said he was Tony.

The factory was busy, full of people this day. But first things first: we went straight to Grizzle Welsch's office, the office that was his while he was alive, anyway. I didn't get a chance to check the place out, though, because when we got inside, Blackarc introduced us to Mr. Kurt Falco, the C.E.O.—that's *C*hief *E*xecutive *O*fficer—of Grizzco Corporation.

The tension was so thick you could have cut it with a chain saw. I half expected somebody to run screaming from the room—me. If looks could kill, Kurt Falco would have cut me dead at twenty paces. He would have made a great vice principal back at school.

I doubt that he would have been interested in a job change, though. With Grizzle Welsch officially gone, Falco was now the big shot in the company—or at least he would be until everything was handed over to me—and he didn't look like the type of guy who handed over *anything* without a fight.

Gulp.

Falco was a very stern-looking man in a very expensive-looking suit. More than stern, he was downright *mean* looking, the kind of guy who only enjoys his day if he runs over a squirrel with his car on the way to work. He was sitting behind the big wood desk—Grizzle's desk—surrounded by four assistants, none of whom seemed happy to see us. The assistants were called—I swear this is true—Mark, Mack, Milt, and Milo. They acted just like robots. Blackarc told them who we were.

Falco accepted the introductions without comment, but then again, he looked like he could have bitten the head off a snake and never changed his expression. He just said, in a very quiet voice, "Well. At last we meet. How do you do?"

I shrugged. "I'm all right, I guess."

Falco smiled. "All right? Yes. You're hardly 'all right,' as you say, but I'll accept that—for now. Milo?"

One of the assistants stepped around the desk, saying, "Mr. Falco is extremely upset about this press conference you have scheduled."

"Upset?" Falco stood up himself, losing his cool. "I am *ticked off,* that's what I am. Blackarc, you have reporters prowling all over this place, asking questions, and I was never notified."

Andy tried to answer. "Mr. Falco, your office was informed by messenger—"

"*I* was never properly told. *I* had no time to prepare. One might almost think you wanted this to be a surprise to me. Well, it won't work, I can assure you of that. Whatever you have planned won't work."

Blackarc was stiff. "We don't have anything planned. We are attempting to comply with Mr. Welsch's wishes."

"Oh . . ." Falco nodded as if the idea had just occurred to him. "You mean the will, of course. The famous Grizzle Welsch will. The document

53

that lets you people go on wasting company money as you have been for years. Well, let me fill you in on something: that will doesn't exist. It never did." Falco sounded very sure of himself.

So did Andy. "There is a will, Mr. Falco. You'll see."

"Oh, I don't doubt that Grizzle claimed it did. But you have to keep in mind that Grizzle wasn't entirely in his right mind towards the end."

"That's not true."

"Isn't it? Are you willing to risk everything on that?"

"Yes, we are."

Falco's neck muscles looked as though they might pop out and injure everyone in the room. He talked, but through clenched teeth. "So. We are just supposed to stand back and hand everything over to this . . . this boy and his car salesman father?"

"Uncle," I said. "He's my uncle."

"What are you people trying to pull?"

Uncle Larry tried to answer. "We're not trying to pull anything, we—"

Falco shook his head. "You surprise me, Blackarc. I've got your file here, you know that?" Falco flipped through the pages on the desk. "You're one of a kind. You speak seven languages, you're a martial arts master, a computer genius. You *invented* the strykometer that's going on the Mars probe. You write poetry, scuba dive, and drive a race car in your spare time. But, like all people, I'm sure you have your price."

Blackarc didn't respond.

I looked over at the bald-headed Blackarc. He did all that stuff? Sheesh, he still looked more like a horror movie bad guy than anything else. What was with him?

Falco continued, "Nobody understands how you think, Blackarc, but that's okay. You had all the makings of a top executive. You could have gone all the way, followed me as director of this company. You still can. Are you going to throw it all away for this?"

Blackarc still didn't say anything.

Nobody said anything.

The tension was just hanging there so I said, "Hey, how about those Cubbies, eh? They're really doing it this year ..."

Falco glared at me. If those eyes were guns then I'd be a memory now, but they weren't. Instead he just signalled his boys and they all left the office together, just like the bad guys from a western movie pushing their way out of a crowded saloon.

I watched them leave. "Nice bunch of boys, huh? We ought to have them over more often, play Monopoly or something."

Andy was moving. She went behind Grizzle's desk and called for me to follow. There was a computer stand built into the side of the desk, and this one *did* have a lock. "Try your code key," she said.

"Okay." I pulled the chain from around my neck and turned the key in the lock. Grizzle appeared on the screen almost immediately, smiling. My friend the ghost. "Well done, Josh, well done. Now you're almost there."

"Almost where?"

"The will, Grizzle." Andy was speaking to the computer now. "Falco is fighting us and we—"

"*Falco.*" Grizzle's face on the screen jumped at that. Now very serious, he said, "Kurt Falco is an extremely dangerous man. At best, misguided, and at worst, evil."

"Oh, yeah?" I asked. "If he's such a creep, why didn't you fire him?"

The computer Grizzle seemed to consider that. "Because Falco was once my friend, a good friend, and I thought I could reform him. Besides, he was the best in the world at what he did, and I could always control him . . ."

"But now you're gone."

"Yes. I'm sorry."

"Sorry doesn't help a whole lot—"

Andy cut me off. "The will, Grizzle. The transition documents. We need them now, to prove that Josh is the heir."

"The will is safe."

"Yes, but where?"

Grizzle just repeated himself: "The will is safe."

All through this, Blackarc was just standing there, saying nothing, but now Andy frowned and said to him, "Something's wrong."

Uncle Larry piped up, his voice a little high. "Wrong?"

"Grizzle . . ." Blackarc spoke very clearly at the TV image. "This is Blackarc. Access your system memory. Where is the will?"

"The will is safe."

"Why can't you tell us where it is?" asked Andy.

"Because . . ." The computer took a moment to think, then Grizzle said, "Because this office is not secure. Someone has it bugged."

Andy slammed a hand down. "Falco!"

I looked around the office. "You mean he's listening to us right now?"

"Yes."

"Falco is a cheesehead!" I yelled. "Falco is a class A supernerd. Falco chews on hot sweaty sneakers! Falco likes to—"

Blackarc had a hand on my shoulder. He shook his head no, and I shut up.

Grizzle was still talking. ". . . if I tell you where the documents are, he could beat you to them. Most likely he would, and that would be the end to this project."

Project? I raised a finger. "Uh, excuse me. I am not a project. I am a junior high school student."

Grizzle and Andy both said at the same time: "Quiet."

I obeyed, but now I was wondering: was I the billionaire here, or not? If I had left the room, I doubt if they would have noticed.

Grizzle went on, giving us instructions. "Do the announcement, do the press conference. Secure your public position. Tell the world. Don't let on to Falco that he has any sort of advantage. I do have a plan."

"*You* have a plan? Grizzle, you've been gone for a year. How can you have a plan?"

"Dead people don't watch much TV. I've been doing nothing but thinking about this. Soon—just as soon as it is safe—I'll tell you where the will and other documents are. Then all you need do is register them with the court, and Falco will be out of the picture."

Uncle Larry had his hands in his pockets, and he asked, "Hey, what happens if you guys don't come up with a will? What then?"

"Not much," answered Blackarc. "We will all lose our careers, you and Josh will be humiliated and stay poor, and there is the possibility that we could all go to jail on charges of fraud."

Uncle Larry nodded. "Humiliated, broke, and in jail. That's all, huh?"

"That's all."

Everybody was looking at me, and I felt very small. That was when the buzzer on the desk went off and, for the first time since I'd known him, Blackarc smiled. "It's show time," he said.

The Press Conference

Flashbulbs were popping and video cameras were whirring all around me. I felt as if I'd just been tossed off of the back of a boat without a life jacket: sink or swim, *just don't say anything stupid.* Feldman, Blackarc, and Andy were trying to rush me through the crowded auditorium, but a woman reporter grabbed me by the shirt sleeve and shoved a big microphone at me. I stopped just to avoid getting hit in the face with it.

"Hey! What's your name?"

"Is it true you're a billionaire?"

"Mr. Blackarc! Mr. Blackarc!"

"Please! How do you know—"

They didn't get a chance to finish their questions, because Feldman pushed them all back out of the way, shoving me up on the stage at the same time. I stumbled and almost fell right off the other side, but Blackarc was there and he snagged me by the collar, keeping me from breaking my neck.

Not that I was really happy about it. The room was full of people, but this wasn't like the deal in the Great Hall; these people definitely weren't members of any Joshua Ellis International Fan Club. They were hard-nosed reporters, no-nonsense people. Or, in other words, they were a bunch of piranha fish ready to chew on my bones if I slipped up and said something stupid.

Half in a panic, I was looking around for an escape. Uncle Larry was nowhere to be seen; there was nobody nearby who might help me get away. I tried talking my way out of it. "Hey, uh, Blackarc, I don't know about all this . . ."

Tap! Tap! Tap! Blackarc ignored me, rapping on the podium microphone. It was definitely on; the volume was cranked up so high his fingertips were rattling the whole building. "Could I have your attention, please?" Blackarc didn't even bother to clear his throat first; he just started talking.

The crowd of reporters started to settle.

"On behalf of Welsch Industries and Grizzco, I'd like to thank you all for coming on such short notice. I have a short statement, after which we will answer questions for twenty minutes."

Twenty minutes? Sheesh, why didn't he just say twenty years?

Blackarc went on. He was reading from a piece of paper, and the paper told the story of me and Grizzle Welsch and, more importantly, Grizzle Welsch and me. Blackarc spoke like Dan Rather reading the news, and it was heavy news indeed. I stood there feeling as if I was on stage for the Christmas play, waiting for my part and not remembering my lines. I was wondering how the reporters were going to handle the big news.

I shouldn't have wondered; the reporters were just like everybody else. They were all in shock at the news that Grizzle was gone—had been dead nearly a year, in fact—and had left everything to me. Lawyers were scurrying around like hamsters in a cage and the Associates—Blackarc's people were gathered up front around me, ready to help handle the nonsense that was sure to follow.

Blackarc was winding down his announcement. "It goes without saying that you would like to hear from Josh, and he's ready to speak to you. I only ask that you remember this is probably more of a shock to him than it is to you, so please, show some sympathy and consideration."

I noticed Falco and his aides then; they were lined up like a row of mean-looking ducks at the back of the auditorium. As crazy as it sounds, the distance made Falco seem even more scary than he had back in Grizzle's office. Looking out across the hall, I could still see his blue eyes, staring right through me. So much for sympathy and consideration.

Blackarc stepped back from the microphone. "Are you ready, Josh?"

I shook my head. "No. No way. Not even close. Forget about it."

"Good enough," he said, pushing me up behind the podium. I was barely tall enough to see over it, but it felt good having a big block of wood between me and the crowd. I didn't know what to do, but everybody else in the room did.

The reporters jumped right in at me, tossing questions around as if I'd been running the company for the last eleven years and doing a lousy job of it. I got the feeling that if there had been rotten fruit and vegetables available—you know, apples, tomatoes, brown heads of lettuce—I would have been wearing them as they pelted me from the audience.

As it was, all they could do was ask questions. They all raised their hands, though, and I got to point out the first guy to ask a question. It was a big guy, with a face like a bull. A bull with a serious attitude problem. I pointed to him because I was afraid if I didn't he might get mad and bite my leg off at the knee.

He said who he was. "Carl Tiller, Associated Press. Justin—"

"Josh," I said. "My name's Josh."

"Oh. I beg your pardon."

"No problem."

"I wanted to ask a question concerning your relationship with Grizzle Welsch."

I shrugged. "He's a nice guy."

" 'Is'?"

"Was, I mean." *Oops.*

"Any reason you said 'is'?" The big bull reporter looked suspicious.

I shrugged again. "I don't think so. I guess it's just hard for me to believe he's dead."

That seemed to work, at least for the moment.

A woman stood up from the *Chicago Tribune* and asked, "How well did you know Grizzle?"

"I didn't. I mean, not that I knew of, anyway. The time I met him he was in disguise."

That interested the reporters; they all wanted to know about the disguise, which led right in to what had happened. I told them the story of the hot dog, but I don't think they believed me. No problem; *I* didn't believe it. Sometimes the truth is like that.

A big man who would have looked good with a big cigar stuck in his face asked the next question. "We're not used to having this sort of access to Grizzco International," he said. "When you're in charge do you plan to allow the press inside more?"

"Why would you want to be inside more?" I asked. "Sheesh, it's a nice day, get outside and do something. You guys play softball?"

They laughed at that. The next person rose to ask a question. "Josh, Grizzco has been accused of totally ignoring environmental issues. Will this change under your leadership?"

I shrugged. "I don't know what you mean."

"Oil spills. Industrial accidents."

"Oh, that stuff . . ." I took a breath. "We won't be doing that anymore."

Again with the laughter. "What?"

"This is the only planet we've got, right?"

"Uh . . . Yes, but how can you just say that you're not going to do that anymore."

I shrugged. "We're going to be more careful."

That was a headline the next day, by the way,

in the *New York Times:* WE'RE GOING TO BE
MORE CAREFUL.

This really got the questions going.

"Won't safety cost you more?"

I shrugged. "So?"

Another headline: *SO?*

"What about nuclear power?"

"I don't like it."

A really thin guy pointed a pencil at me; the
pencil was *almost* as skinny as he was. "So will
Grizzco abandon its Southridge project?"

"Is that a nuke plant?"

"Yes."

I waved my hand: "Color it gone."

Now the crowd was with me, laughing. It was
just like the scene in the Great Hall, except
instead of Miss Lisa looking at me as though she
hated me, it was Falco handling that role. He
and his guys stood grimly in the back, looking as
if he'd love nothing more than to drive a wooden
stake through my evil heart. When I made the
'color it gone' crack, though, they did worse than
just give me dirty looks. They all stormed out of
the hall.

Sorry about that, dude, I thought. (Ha, ha!)

"What about the people who lost their homes to
your northern Michigan project?" This was from a
woman reporter who still seemed skeptical.

I looked at Blackarc a second, then said, "I
don't know anything about that."

She explained. "Your company forced several
dozen homeowners in Michigan to sell to you, so
that you could build a massive project up there.

64

The project has been cancelled, but now Grizzco still intends to knock down their houses to make room for a new shopping center and parking lot."

I shrugged. "They can have their houses back," I said. "How many more mall pretzel places do we need?"

Headline: HOW MANY MALL PRETZEL PLACES DO WE NEED?

The line of questioning changed a little. A reporter from Dallas asked what I was going to do with the money, in general.

I thought for a minute, then decided. "I'm going to get some baseball cards. Then I want to buy the Chicago Cubs."

Again they were all amused. "Why?"

"I want to give the manager a few weeks off."

Everybody laughed.

I explained myself: "Everybody always fires the manager when things are bad. Maybe he only needs some time off, a vacation, maybe. Who knows?"

Headline: WHO KNOWS?

"Are you going to be doing a lot of company reorganizing, Josh?"

"Not as much as some."

"Tell us about your uncle."

I shrugged. "He sells cars."

"New or used?"

"Depends on who you ask."

"Do you have a girlfriend, Josh?"

"Do pigs fly?"

"So you *don't* have a girlfriend."

"No. But I *do* have a flying pig."

Laughs. Laughs. More laughs.

"Josh, what grade did you get in math last year?"

"Next question!" I yelled.

More laughter.

Sheesh, I thought, very pleased with myself, I should be a comedian.

I found out way too late that being funny was never the main idea . . .

Miss Lisa

"Well," said Andy, spreading her hands, "All in all, I think it went great."

"Yeah," said Uncle Larry, still a little green from the trip back. "All but the chopper ride home. How come you guys keep letting Josh fly? He can't even ride his bike without falling off."

We were in Grizzle's study and everybody else was drinking coffee. Me they handed a bottle of soda pop, without an opener. It wasn't a twistoff, either; I almost ripped off my hand trying to open it. Blackarc ignored all this talk. He just said, "Well, it's begun, anyway."

"What's begun?" I asked, ready to bash the bottle against the desk.

"The great adventure."

"Some adventure," I said. "I thought at first all those reporters were going to lynch me."

Andy gave me a pat on the back, saying, "Don't worry about it. You did great."

Blackarc turned to me, changing the subject. He said, "Decisions have to be made on day-to-day operations."

"That's true," I said, giving up my struggle. "First of all, we need to buy a bottle opener."

Nobody even heard me. They were all chattering back and forth, especially Andrea Charlene Hampton Everett Morse. She was saying, "If we don't take action right away, Falco will, and that will only make him look more and more like the one in charge."

"We still need that will and stuff," Uncle Larry reminded everybody. Everybody but me, of course. I was the odd man—the odd *kid*—out.

"He's right," Andy said, nodding. "I'm sure Falco is out there right now with a dozen lawyers, all trying to find a way to pull the rug out from under us."

Us? Nobody was even looking at me. I wasn't even a person anymore. I was a subject, like something you studied at school: history, math, geography, and Josh.

They were all studying me hard but I thought hey, who's the billionaire here, anyway?

They kept talking, but I wasn't listening as much. Actually I was getting bored. Usually on weekends I get out and do stuff, play some softball, or basketball, or ride bikes, *anything*. All these people did was plot and scheme, which was all right, I guess, but it definitely got old real quick. If this was the rich man's game, I was definitely going to have to change the rules some.

I was wondering whether I could get away with sneaking out and exploring stuff. Good stuff, neat stuff. Maybe go find Mike the pilot and learn some helicopter stuff. Trying not to attract notice,

I wandered out of the room. They didn't even notice me go; they were all still caught up in their strategy session.

Three Acres. What a place, I was thinking, and that was just the main house, nobody had let me see anything else yet. The hallways were as long as a football field, almost, and lined with sculptures and statues. The floors were slick tile—freshly waxed, I guess—and it was a good thing I wasn't walking around in socks or else I probably would have slipped and broken my neck and. . . .

"Hello, Josh," I said out loud. "Wait a minute . . ."

I stopped and took off my sneakers, then walked around in a quick little circle. It was almost like walking on skates, I was *almost* off balance every step I took. Great.

I looked ahead of me. Nothing but room.

Uncle Larry, Blackarc, and the others were discussing important things I guess, but for me, it was time to make wax-skating history.

Yeah, I thought, backing up as far as I could, until my back brushed up against a wall. There was a bronze suit of armor standing in the corner and I looked over and said to it, "Watch this, guy: Joshua Ellis, Olympic champion."

The suit of armor didn't say anything, which almost surprised me, considering the house I was in. I took off, getting a good running start as I ran past the paintings and sculptures. Then, suddenly, I stopped.

Of course I didn't really *stop;* that was the whole idea. When I locked my knees and put on

69

the brakes I started to slide. Leaving my stomach behind I slid forward, fighting for my balance and picking up speed until finally I slipped and fell on my rear, laughing.

"Hey, not bad!" I said, looking behind me. I'd slid a good ten or twelve feet. I could do better than that.

I needed some way to measure myself, though, to figure out how far I was skating. It didn't take me too long to figure out a system. I checked out the closest head: SOCRATES, said the bust. Okay, this time I needed to slide further than Socrates.

And I did. The next time I went I got as far as Plato. There was a full statue of Abraham Lincoln at the end of the hall, and I was pretty sure I could make that, if I got my speed up and timed my braking just right . . .

It was hard working up speed on the slippery floor, but I kept getting better and better. On my fourth attempt, I was totally out of control when I went into my slide, a rocket shooting down the hall with nothing to stop me but Lincoln's outstretched arms. Which meant, I realized too late, that I was probably going to kill myself doing this.

Oh well, I thought. The space program has its dangers, too. I was about to close my eyes and ride it out when, of course, Miss Lisa walked around the corner right into my way. Caught up in a book she was reading, she wasn't aware that she was about to get clobbered.

I tried to stop myself, I swear I did: "Whoa,

whoa, *whoa!*" Putting on the brakes didn't help; there were no brakes. I just flapped my arms up and down like penguin flippers and went tumbling right into the poor girl. She heard me yelling and looked up, but she looked up 'way too late. Next thing either of us knew, we were tangled up together and rolling end over end.

We made it to Lincoln's feet, though. Not bad.

Miss Lisa wasn't quite as pleased as I was. As a matter of fact, she grabbed her book and hit me over the head with it. "Ow!" I said. Fortunately, it was a paperback.

"Are you *crazy?*" she asked, pushing me away and trying to get up. "Are you totally crazy?"

"No," I said, trying to explain myself. "I was wax-skating and I—"

"*Wax*-skating?"

"Yeah, and I—"

Bam! She hit me over the head with the book again.

"Ow! Hey, what are you doing?"

"Nothing much," she said, looking ready to hit me again. "Just trying to let the world's newest billionaire know he just can't go around sliding into anybody he wants to."

"I said I was sorry."

"Yeah. Right." On her feet now, Miss Lisa started to leave.

"Hey, wait a minute," I said. "Where are you going?"

"What's it to you?"

"Nothing, excuse me for living. I just wondered. I'm bored. What's that you're reading?"

"Poetry. You have something against poetry?"

I was rubbing my head. "No, I'm just glad it wasn't a big dictionary or something. You would have cracked my skull. How come you hate me so much?"

"Because you're rude and crazy."

I raised a finger. "That's not true. You hated me long before you knew I was rude and crazy."

I had her on the spot. She sighed, looked around, and said, "I'm just worried, that's all. *We're* worried."

"About what?"

"Three Acres. All the families here. All our friends."

"So why are you worried?"

"Because Grizzle left it all to you."

"Oh ..." So that was it, I thought. She was jealous.

Miss Lisa came back as though she were reading my mind. "No, we're not jealous. The problem is everybody thinks you and your uncle might sell us out without even knowing what you were doing."

"What do you mean, sell you out?"

"Falco wants to tear down Three Acres."

"That's true," I said. "But Falco's just a really fun guy all around."

She looked at me funny, not realizing that I was kidding. I told her not to worry about it. "I wouldn't sell Falco a glass of water if his nose was on fire."

She nodded. Finally she said, "We saw you on TV."

"How'd I look?"

"Short."

I rolled my eyes. "Wonderful."

"So what are you doing wandering around? Besides trying to kill people, I mean?"

Shrugging, I said, "I don't know. Everybody was ignoring me and it was getting kind of depressing. I was thinking about maybe going to talk to Grizzle for a while."

Miss Lisa's eyes went wide. "I heard about that, but I didn't think it was true. Can you really talk to Grizzle? Even though he's dead?"

"*Especially* because he's dead. I only talked to him once before, and that was just to buy him a hot dog."

Miss Lisa just looked at me a minute. "You lead a very strange life, you know that?"

"Yeah, I guess I do. Sort of," I said. I explained how it worked, and she got excited. At Three Acres, Grizzle was a hero to everybody, I guess. Everybody but Blackarc, who had no heroes. Miss Lisa said, "May I try? May I talk to him? Please?"

I thought about it a second. "Are you going to hit me with that book again?"

She blushed. "No."

"Okay, come on."

The study was full, so I was going to take her to the computer station in my room, via the talking elevator, but the stupid machine had other ideas. "Kindly call out your floors, please."

"It's me," I said. "Josh."

73

"Oh," said the elevator, perking up. "Hello, how are you, Master Joshua? Is that weasel Norman with you?"

"No, this is Miss Lisa."

"Good. Things go so much easier when he's not standing around, complaining about something all the time and—"

"Elevator?"

"Oh, sorry. I do get carried away. And you know what they say: he who gets carried away, sometimes gets carried away. It's like my dad used to say—my dad was an express elevator in the Empire State building—he used to say to me—"

"Elevator."

"Yes, sir?"

"Can we just go up to my room, please?"

"Sure, no problem," said the elevator, closing its doors. That's when it dropped like a stone.

Miss Lisa and I screamed together: "AHHHHH!"

Here we go, I thought.

The elevator actually dropped so fast our feet left the floor and we had to grab hold of the handrail to keep from slamming into the ceiling. "Hey!" I yelled. "Hey! What are you doing?"

The elevator laughed: "Going *dowwwwwwn!*"

"Why?"

BAM! We stopped just as suddenly as we dropped, and Miss Lisa and I again fell to the floor together in a heap. She shoved me back and said, "Get off of my leg."

This wasn't my fault. I tried to say so.

74

"Subbasement," said the elevator, very calmly. "I hope you both enjoyed the ride."

"Hey, elevator," I said.

"Yes, sir?"

"I suppose you think this is funny."

"Nope, uh-uh, no way. Well, a little, I guess."

"How about if I get an axe and start reprogramming you a little?"

"Sorry."

The doors opened. We were in the Batcave.

Sort of. We were in that sort of deep, out-of-the-way place, and we were definitely surrounded by all sorts of gadgets. It was like a scene out of a science fiction movie. Before us was a round room, the heart of the machine, the home of the computer. Things were clicking and buzzing, lights of a dozen different colors were flashing, and a dead guy was asking us if we wanted a Coke.

Miss Lisa's eyes were wide again. She whispered: "Grizzle?"

The computer whirred, memory racing, and his deep voice—in stereo all around us now—said, "Have you got your code key, Josh?"

I nodded absently, still looking around from the safety—I thought—of the elevator. "Yeah. It's on my person."

"Use it to identify yourself at the terminal," he said. "Then we can get started."

I stepped forward, pulling Miss Lisa with me. "What is this place?"

The computer whirred. "I'm sorry," he said. "I

cannot respond without the code key. Would you like a Coke?"

There was a soda machine across from us, fitted in between two computer banks. Above it was a sign that said, SPILL SODA ON THE EQUIPMENT AT YOUR OWN RISK.

I pulled the code key out from around my neck, asking Grizzle, "Did you bring us down here or is the computer just a jerk?"

"I'm sorry," he said. "I cannot respond without the code key. Would you like a Coke?"

I got the point.

"What's that?" asked Miss Lisa as I pulled out the code key; I explained as I used it. Immediately, the computer was happy and Grizzle was chatting with us. "How did it go?" he asked. "I monitored the press conference. How did you feel about it?"

"I felt like a shark was chewing on my foot. It sure wasn't much fun. I don't have to do that again, do I?"

"I don't think so," he said. There were a bunch of switched-off television sets built into the wall, right in front of two chairs. These sets came on now, all at once. There were five of them, and three showed the action going on inside of the study. Andy, Uncle Larry, Norman, and Feldman were still talking as Blackarc stood quietly by.

I was surprised. "You bug yourself?"

Grizzle answered from one of the other monitors, saying, "I don't invade anyone else's privacy, but they are talking in my—*our*—study."

I reached down to the control panel. There was

a volume switch, and I turned it up and listened for a while. Mostly it was more of the same, plotting and planning against Falco while Blackarc listened without saying too much. I turned the sound down again.

"What's the problem?" asked Miss Lisa, looking puzzled. "I thought you were in charge. I thought the money was definitely yours."

I explained the problems, at least so far as I understood them. While I talked I fell back in one of the seats before the control panel. Things in my life were so weird, and I didn't even know how to take them. I was just about ready to dump this whole billionaire concept and go back to the trailer court. The only fun part had been flying the helicopter, anyway. That and wax-skating in the hall, which only got me into trouble.

Grizzle wasn't much help, either. He announced, "There's something worse than all this, you know."

I had my head in my hands. "What could possibly be worse?"

Miss Lisa knew. She smiled. "You 've got to go back to school tomorrow."

My New School

I won't bother to whine. (Okay, so I am going to whine a little, but I promise not to go on and on about it.) All I'll say is the first thing they told me about my new school was that it really *was* my new school. I owned it.

Norman came and woke me up in the morning—Norman, the guy who couldn't get along with the elevator (and I was beginning to understand why. Going up to bed I'd taken the stairs. They were glad to see me, and we talked some baseball before I had to get going. But that's another story.).

Norman introduced me around. There were six different staff members assigned to see me off to school in the morning, people who obviously either had nothing better to do, or else were being well paid to aggravate and make me crazy. The weirdest of them was the tall and skinny guy who said he was Max, my valet.

"My *what?*"

"Your valet. I assist you with your wardrobe." He then showed me three different outfits, none

78

of which I would have worn to a zoo picnic on the planet Mars, much less the first day at a new school. "What happened to my old clothes?" I asked. "The ones from the trailer?"

"Mr. Blackarc ordered you new clothes more befitting a young man of your station."

"Station? Space station, maybe." I nodded. "Great. So where are my old clothes?"

"I'm afraid I took the liberty of having them burned."

"Burned?"

"Yes, with gasoline, I believe. There was very little choice; the clothes in question were hardly suitable for a school of Van Tark Academy's status."

"Oh. Right. Status, I *do so* keep forgetting." I pointed out the selection of clothes Max was offering me. "Don't you have anything normal in the closet? Those are suits. I'm not a stockbroker, you know. I've never worn a tie in my life."

"Well . . . you *do* realize Van Tark Academy has a dress code?"

Van Tark Academy? This place they were sending me did not exactly sound like Disneyland. This place sounded more like the sort of school of my worst non-billionaire nightmares. "You mean they say I have to wear a suit?"

" 'Collared shirt and necktie,' is the regulation, I believe." Max was still arranging clothes on my bed for me, awaiting my choice.

"That's crazy. They'll never last."

"The school has lasted for one hundred and forty years."

"So? That doesn't mean they'll make one forty-one."

"I should hope they do," said Max. "Especially since you own the school."

"What?" That one really threw me. "How the heck can a kid own a school?"

Max explained it to me. "Oh. That's how. Okay. I just figured a kid owning a school would be sort of against the law or something."

I finally got dressed, but it was a compromise. I wore the collared shirt and jacket, but stuck the blue tie in my pocket. Then I went down to breakfast.

The next two guys I met were the cook and the waiter. The waiter took my order and the cook brought it out to me. "I usually eat in the kitchen," I said. "A bowl of cornflakes over the sink, so if I spill milk it doesn't get all over the floor. Plus, when I'm finished I can just dump what's left into the garbage disposal. You guys don't have any Ratman cereal, do you? It's little chocolate bits shaped like—"

I didn't finish. They were looking at me as though I'd just fallen out of a tree, so I said, "Well, you probably don't want to know what Ratman cereal is shaped like."

They seemed shocked at the thought. "Grizzle would never have heard of such a thing."

"I don't know. You guys would be surprised what Grizzle's heard of."

They didn't understand what I was talking about, and I didn't explain. Instead I asked, "Where's my uncle?"

The two guys looked at each other. "Uh . . . he's with Mr. Blackarc."

"Oh, yeah? What's he doing with Blackarc?"

"Morning exercises, I believe."

"Which means?"

"He's screaming, begging, and pleading for mercy."

They weren't kidding. Uncle Larry was so stiff from trying to keep up with Blackarc he had a hard time walking the rest of the week.

I was taken to school by limo which, as a way of travelling, does have certain built-in advantages. For one thing you can drink orange juice and watch TV on your way, which I did. The news on TV was about me.

Well, not exactly about me.

They were calling me the richest kid in the world, and when I looked at my glass of orange juice and the limo I was riding in with Feldman my bodyguard, it wasn't so hard to believe.

Still, life is life. I still had an uncle who was a loudmouth klutzy coward, I now had not just one but dozens of people trying to control my life, and I was still wondering about Grizzle, the dead guy who still talked to me. What of that?

The next face on TV was Falco. He looked very unhappy, and he was facing his own set of reporters.

"Turn up the sound," I said, and Feldman did.

They were talking to Falco about my claim to the money, and he just shook his head. "Nothing has been determined yet. All of that is still up in the air."

A reporter asked, "Is the board of directors planning to fight?"

Falco shrugged. "Obviously, I cannot speak for the directors, but to me there are some . . . uh, questions which haven't been answered yet. They say they have the original will and execution documents, but I've yet to see them."

The will. There it was again. Grizzle still wouldn't tell me where it was, not yet. He was waiting until the last minute for some reason, playing some game I didn't understand.

They asked Falco one last question: "What about Three Acres? What about the Grizzle Welsch Foundation?"

Falco just smiled, waved at the reporters, climbed into his own limo, and rode off.

"That," I said to Feldman, "is one ugly dude."

"Yes, sir."

"I'm serious. What do you think of that mustache? Looks like hamster fur."

Feldman laughed, and I finished my orange juice. We were pulling up to the school.

The school grounds, actually, since the Van Tark Academy consisted of several buildings on an estate. It was nowhere near the size of Three Acres, of course, but it was big enough to make a person feel small. Especially when that person knew it was supposed to be his new school.

"This may not be the best idea anybody around here has ever had," I said after we'd stopped and Feldman had my door open.

William C. Decker disagreed.

Mr. Decker was the Dean of Students at the

Academy, which must be something like a vice principal, because he sure acted like one. The only problem was he ranted on and on like some U.S. Marines drill sergeant before one of his assistants had the chance to tell him that not only was I a new student, but I also was his new boss.

He still ranted on for a while. The other kids were already in class, but they—Mr. Decker and a woman assistant—took me around and showed me things. The first big thing I noticed was that the padlock was missing from my locker. "Hey, where's my lock?"

"What?"

"My locker lock. I'm not putting my stuff in there without a lock. It'll all get swiped."

Mr. Decker rolled his eyes at me. "No one is going to 'swipe' anything. This isn't that sort of school."

"Oh, right. Tell me another one."

Mr. Decker did, saying, "Here at the Academy we have a strict honor code. Every student swears by it: 'I will not lie, cheat, or steal. Nor will I tolerate anyone who does.' "

"What do you mean, 'tolerate'? You mean snitch on somebody? Tattletale?"

" 'Tattletale'?"

"Look, I'd still like to have a lock on my locker."

"What?"

"Just remember who signs your paychecks from now on," I said. It was mean, I know. I have to confess I was in a bad mood and I didn't stop there. "I own this school, right?"

"Yes, but Mister Welsch—"

"Mister Welsch won't be around. I'm the new honcho."

"Yes, but—"

"No more but. Here's the deal: first off, the dress code is cancelled. It's history, a memory. Next, we need to mellow out. This place looks like a cross between a church, a hospital, and a cemetery. We need to repaint."

Decker's brain was bubbling. I could feel it.

I was still thinking, though. I asked, "Does this school have dances?"

"No."

"It does now."

I caught Decker's woman assistant smiling. So did he; she dropped it right away. I wasn't even close to being done, but I could see the guy was going to have a stroke. "Some advice," I said to Mr. Decker. "Next time make sure you know who you're yelling at!"

Blackarc

Okay, so I was depressed. A little.

I got up really early the next morning, really early, 'way ahead of any of the staff. It was the only way to get any peace, to be sure nobody was going to pounce and ask if I wanted anything.

And for probably the first time since I became a billionaire, I didn't want anything.

Except a little advice, maybe.

When I found Blackarc, he was acting almost as loony as I felt.

He was down in the gym. I'd wandered down there thinking maybe I'd grab a basketball and shoot some baskets, but I heard the noises before I even made it out of the locker room. At first I didn't know what was going on, though, so I took it slow and easy and peeked around the corner.

Blackarc was dressed all in white, in a padded fencer's outfit, and he was sword fighting with himself.

Sword fighting. Alone.

I stood there, back where he couldn't see me, and watched for a while. It was as though he were fighting some invisible guy. But here's the weird part: he was losing.

Seriously. He was beating himself!

Not that he wasn't trying his best against his other self, the one that was winning (this gets weird, I know, but hang in there with me). Sweat covered his forehead, and every time he lunged forward he kept forcing himself back, warding off invisible blows. I guess he was being so badly beaten by himself that he lost his balance for a second, because he almost slipped and fell. But he caught himself in time, and lunged forward with a desperate grunt, swinging his sword right and left.

"I have you!" he cried out, making his move, but just as he started to turn he suddenly froze. He stopped and sighed, dropping his arms to his side.

"Well done," he started to say to himself, but I guess he sensed my presence then, because he turned and acknowledged me with a nod and greeting. "Ah, Josh. Good morning."

I said hello to him and asked, "What the heck are you doing?"

"Fencing."

"Yeah, but how can you fight yourself?"

"Mental discipline."

"Huh?"

Blackarc explained. "Few people can actually do this. It's like playing chess with oneself, only more physical. You must always anticipate your own moves, guess your own reactions, and in that millisecond attempt to counter your own moves and reactions, and in that same millisecond try to fool yourself again."

"That sounds a little crazy."

"Yes, perhaps it is. But it teaches you to think on your feet. Come, try it."

"What? Fence with you?"

"No, fence with yourself."

"Huh?"

"As I've just said. I'll show you."

I thought a second then shrugged. "Why not? I've seen it in the movies, I guess."

"Indeed. Let's see what sort of a swordsman you are."

"Why? Is this like a billionaire sport or something?"

Blackarc almost smiled. Almost. "Or something," he said.

He brought me forward, showed me how to position my feet. "Balance is the most important thing," he said. "Bend your knees."

I did.

"Good. Your knees bend, you bounce. The trick is never to fall down. If you fall, you die."

"Die?"

Blackarc tapped me in the center of the chest.

I looked at the tip of the sword I was holding, made the connection. "Oh."

Blackarc went on, showing me how to thrust (push the sword at the other guy) and parry (knock his sword away with mine) and other such nonsense. Pretty soon I was just about ready to battle somebody, but I didn't understand exactly what Blackarc meant for me to do about fighting myself.

At first I tried faking it, pretending I was in some scene from an old pirate movie, swinging around and fighting the bad guys, but Blackarc cut me off with a yell.

"No!"

I stopped. "What's wrong?"

"Where's your mind? What are you thinking about?"

"Uh . . . saving the princess," I admitted.

"I thought as much. Mental discipline, remember. You have to concentrate, attack the enemy—and remember, your worst enemy is often yourself."

I nodded. Right. If you were your own worst enemy, then Blackarc had to contend with a big bald guy, but all I had to fight was a twerp seventh grader. No problem.

"En garde," said Blackarc.

"I've heard that before. What does it mean?"

"Stand ready."

I raised the sword, tried to imagine myself—another self—standing in front of me, ready to fight. It wasn't easy, and I had to use a lot of imagination, but I could almost do it. Almost.

"Okay," I muttered under my breath. I wanted to beat myself now, just to prove to Blackarc that I could do it.

I didn't, though, not that morning. I didn't win to myself, I lost to myself (this gets crazy, I know), but that was only my first lesson. I started getting up early mornings, and hanging out with

Blackarc after school; he taught me a lot of things. Like that old guy in *Star Wars,* Blackarc was passing along his wisdom to me.

He taught me how to fence, and told me to read more. Especially history. "If you can learn from the past mistakes of others, you'll save yourself a lot of trouble in this life," he said.

He also taught me about the business end of some things, and when I was called on to make a decision—as I was every once in awhile now—he helped me by giving me choices. He never told me what to do; he always gave me at least two choices and then let me make my own decision. "You have to learn leadership, learn to be a good executive."

I saw all of Three Acres, which, as I said, was more like a small town than just a house or estate. Everybody who lived there had a little personal project going. One guy was an astronomer, and he had a bunch of telescopes aimed up at the sky from a balcony on the house. "What are you looking for?" I asked.

"Comets."

I nodded. "Found any?"

"Seventeen so far."

"Wow."

Another guy was a writer, researching a book he was doing about talking to bees. To do this, he kept a beehive out in the yard somewhere. "We can learn a lot from the insect," he said. "But first we need to talk to them."

"Right."

There was a woman working on a time machine

and a couple of guys trying to discover the meaning of life. And they all had their families, their kids with them. We were surrounded by scientists, and artists, and painters (that explained all the paintings and sculptures and stuff around the main house). Everything was wild, yes, but I didn't think these people were crazy; I thought they were all great. "What's wrong with being weird?" I asked Blackarc.

"Nothing at all," he said. "Everything in the universe must balance. That's all."

He told me a lot, but one thing Blackarc would never talk about was Grizzle Welsch.

"Why not?" I'd ask. "Did he mess you over or something?"

"No. We got along quite well."

"Don't you ever talk to him on the computer?"

Blackarc shook his big, bald head. "No."

"Why not?"

"Because I knew him well when he was alive. To you, Grizzle lives within the machine, and so be it. But to me, it's just a dry recording of a man who's gone."

"Do you miss him?"

"Sometimes yes. Sometimes no."

"What do you mean?"

"Things. Things I have to do . . ." His voice trailed off.

"Like what?"

Blackarc wouldn't say; he ended the talk. He usually did when we got onto Grizzle.

Andy was my lawyer, as I've said, and every once in a while she would explain to Blackarc and Uncle Larry what the current situation was concerning the money. I'd be totally ignored, and, usually, I'd just get up and leave. I talked to Grizzle on the computer, and he always told me not to concern myself, because plans and strategies were underway. He wouldn't tell me where the will and other documents were, just that they were close. He said he would tell me when it was safe, when we could deliver them to the court without fear of anything going wrong.

Meanwhile, we were guests of the computer. It made all the decisions for the company and the house, and I had the code key to make those decisions. I was boss; it just wasn't official yet.

Whatever that meant.

Miss Lisa wasn't impressed. She still didn't trust me, and wanted to know what Grizzle was up to, as if I knew but was keeping it from everybody just to make life more exciting. "Sheesh," I said, "I can't keep my uncle out of trouble, and you think I'm plotting and planning like some evil genius out of a spy movie."

"You do spend a lot of time down in the subbasement."

"Yeah," I admitted. "Sometimes it's the only place around here where a person can get some peace and quiet."

She didn't believe me. "I think you're up to something and just won't admit it."

"If I was up to something I would be the first person to admit it. Believe me."

I don't think she did.

Well, whatever.

When things got too crazy and tense, Blackarc and I fought. Not with each other. I had my own sword and fencing suit now, and in the evenings or early morning hours we would go down to the gym and battle ourselves.

"Fencing is not just a sport," Blackarc said. "Fencing is an attitude. A way of carrying yourself. You must forget about the sword. You must use your entire body as your weapon, as your instrument. Use your oneself to beat your otherself."

"Right," I said.

"Instinct," he warned. "When your body becomes the weapon, instinct becomes your best friend, your ally."

"Ally, right."

I have to admit, I started to kind of like it, trying to outguess myself. If you think that's easy, try it. I mean *really* try it, no cheating. And if you can honestly not cheat yourself . . .

I was jumping around like a complete maniac, swinging the sword and trying to catch myself in a mistake. And whenever I did catch myself in a mistake, I blocked off my own attack, kept the sword from getting near the big red heart that was sewn on the front of my white fencing suit.

It was a battle. Half of me wanted to win, and the other half desperately did not want to lose. I did my best both ways, trying to think, and think, and think and—

A look of total surprise came over my face as I lunged forward with the sword. My heart was beating very fast and for a second I thought I might faint.

Blackarc waited, watching.

"I didn't know I was going to do that!" I said. "I did it! I beat myself! I caught myself totally by surprise! I really beat myself!"

Blackarc nodded, ever so slowly. "Well done," he said, looking proud of me. "Very well done."

The Proposal

The next day wouldn't have been bad, except for the fact that I was hit over the head and kidnapped. Two things made it even worse: one, Uncle Larry was with me when it happened and two, the kidnappers offered to pay me the ransom if I would just go away. Far, far away.

I was kidnapped—as I often seem to be these days—right after school. Which was too bad, because I was like a hero there after changing the rules. Now the place was less like a concentration camp and more like a regular school. Even some of the teachers liked it, although they couldn't say so in front of Mr. Decker.

I made a couple of friends there, even though they were all rich kids. (What am I saying? I was a rich kid too; I even came to and from school in a limo. Sheesh . . .)

All in all, though, despite all my changes—and it was definitely weird owning the place—no matter what I did, it was still a school. The biggest difference I saw between it and my old school was that most of the kids were very serious, studying hard (or at least harder than I was). Why bother, I wondered.

"You don't know my dad," said one kid, a boy called Wheaties because he was a pretty big guy, at least as big and strong as Lyle. "With the money he pays to send me here, he expects to see good grades."

"Yeah, but you're rich. What's the point of getting good grades?"

Wheaties shrugged. "I don't know. For my future, I guess. I have to get into a good college. Life's a rat race, remember."

"Yeah, but you already beat all the other rats. Why are you still racing?"

He shrugged again. I couldn't get my point across, and maybe I shouldn't have been trying. They were probably right; I was probably wrong.

Anyway, school was still school, except the lunches were worse and my ride was better. I strolled out to my limo and opened the back door—I'd long since told Feldman not to bother opening doors for me, it was stupid—but I stopped, because it wasn't *my* limo. I recognized the guys inside right away: Mark, Mack, and Milt, assistants to the great Mr. Falco. This was not a good sign.

"Oops," I said, backing up and wondering where the other guy was. That was when Milo grabbed me from behind and shoved me inside, hitting me on the head as he did it.

"Ow!" I said as they pulled the door shut and drove off. "This is getting kind of old, guys."

They said nothing.

"Would I be right if I guessed we're not going to the movies?"

Still nothing.

"Oh, well. Life got ugly and the guys around me got uglier . . ."

Another group of guys had been sent to snatch Uncle Larry, I guess, and we were brought together in Falco's big office, where he had his own computer terminal. The computer wasn't in use, though, and I wondered if they could use it without my code key.

Not that it mattered.

I got nervous right away when Falco, seated behind a desk even bigger than Grizzle's, started off by being too polite. "Good afternoon," he said. "I'm afraid I must apologize."

"Oh, yeah?" I looked around. There was all kinds of stuff in the big office: globes, models, sculptures. I started wandering around, checking it all out.

"Yes. I needed to speak with you both privately, without any reporters or lawyers around."

"You mean Andy?"

"Yes, that's right."

"Why?"

Falco folded his hands together and said, "I have a proposal for you."

"I'm a little young to get married."

Falco grimaced, unimpressed with the joke. He seemed disgusted with what he had to say. "I am prepared to offer a settlement."

"What?" I was busy playing with a model airplane I pulled off of the bookshelf. The wing came

96

off in my hand. I dropped it and picked up a small globe.

Uncle Larry was now seated, and chewing on a pipe. He didn't smoke, but somewhere along the line he got the idea that carrying a pipe made him look intelligent, thoughtful. He posed with his pipe and said, "What are we talking about?"

Falco explained. "We could keep fighting this. We could tie you up in court for years, bury you in legal expenses you couldn't possibly pay. And you would lose. In court, your type always lose. Surely you know that. We—Grizzo International, the directors—are prepared to offer you ten million dollars to drop your claim to any portion of Grizzle Welsch's estate."

"Ulp!" Uncle Larry almost swallowed his pipe.

"The money will be yours. Now. Immediately. No big legal problems. You can do with it as you will. We're willing to write off that much in order to end this now, out of the newspapers. We'll write you a check today."

I thought about that. "Who would wind up running Grizzco? You?"

"The board of directors."

"I don't think that's what Grizzle wanted."

"GRIZZLE WELSCH IS DEAD!" Furious, Falco was on his feet and slamming a fist down on the desk. "Dead is dead, who cares what he wants . . . wanted, I mean!"

I didn't answer. Instead I asked, "So what happens to Three Acres?"

"That's none of your concern."

"I want to know."

Falco raised an eyebrow. "Why?"

Good question. I was thinking of Miss Lisa—and Andy, and Norman, and the others, but I didn't even really know why. I looked at Falco and said, "That's none of *your* concern."

"Three Acres remains a Grizzco asset," he said. "The staff is to be dismissed, the grounds leveled, and the land properly developed."

"Properly developed? What the heck does that mean?"

"Sign the papers and I'll explain the American business system to you."

"I don't think so."

"Josh . . ." Uncle Larry sounded *very* nervous.

Falco didn't blink. He just said, "What if I make it twelve million? You could support almost all the people from Three Acres on that."

I was thinking about Grizzle. He'd gone to an awful lot of trouble to bring me into this, to make me his heir, and I couldn't help but think it had to do with more than money. "No way," I said. "Sorry."

"Fifteen million."

Uncle Larry choked. "Josh, think about this a second."

"Yes, think," said Falco. "Don't you realize the legal resources I have at my disposal? I've got an army of lawyers. Even if you could afford it, you'd lose, and even if you won you'd be ninety before you saw a dime. I'm offering you, in cash . . . *twenty million dollars*."

Uncle Larry looked as if he was going to faint. "I gotta sit down," he said.

"You are sitting down."

"I gotta sit more down."

Twenty million. I did stop for a second then, because Falco was right on one account. I could probably have taken care of all the people from Three Acres with that much. But ... "It isn't right," I said.

"What isn't right? The figure? The amount? How much do you want? I am willing to negotiate."

"No," I said. "None of this is right. Grizzle wanted me to have this, to take over in his place, and there must have been a reason."

"Sentimental tripe."

"Maybe. But maybe that's why he left it to me and not to you."

"You'll have to be able to prove that. I'm not so sure you can."

I turned to Uncle Larry and said, "Hey, we don't need their twenty million dollars, do we?"

He didn't say anything.

He *couldn't* say anything.

I think he was in shock.

Falco was overconfident, though. I knew that, because I had Blackarc on my side, and I said so. "You guys just don't know what you're up against."

Falco just shook his head. "I've got to hand it to you; you've both got nerve." He smiled, the same sort of a smile a shark might give you just before he bites into your leg. "It takes a lot of nerve to go head-to-head with the big boys. And I'm the biggest boy on the block."

Maybe, I thought. But obviously he hasn't met Lyle.

Falco aimed a finger at me, and if it had been · a gun, he would have needed a new carpet. "Do you want to go to jail? Is that it?"

"Hey, you guys came to us."

"Oh, yes." Falco nodded, looking at some papers before him. "I'm fully aware that some of our people are involved in this, this . . . *scheme*. The 'Associates,' I believe they call themselves. I know all about them and their little games out at Three Acres."

"You do, huh?"

"Yes. *My* man Blackarc has kept me informed every step of the way."

That stopped me cold. "*Your* man Blackarc?"

"Why yes, of course." Falco grinned. Reaching forward on the desk, he pressed a buzzer and the familiar voice answered, "Yes?"

"Come in, please," said Falco. He kept talking to us. "How else was I supposed to keep tabs on everyone? Business is politics, after all."

Before I could respond, the door opened and Blackarc came in. He closed it behind him and walked over to stand beside the desk.

I could hardly think. I looked over at Blackarc and he turned away. For the first time since I first laid eyes on the big bald-headed guy, he lost his nerve and couldn't look back at me.

"What's going on, Blackarc?" I asked. "What is all this?"

"Take the money," said Falco. "This is the best and last offer you're going to hear from me. From now on I play hardball, and you'll never know where I'm going to hit you."

"Forget you," I said. I walked right over to Blackarc. "I thought we were friends."

He said nothing.

"I trusted you. You taught me all that stuff, how to fence, everything. You were even teaching me how to think for myself."

Still Blackarc said nothing.

Falco did, though. He said, "I'll give you both until morning to make up your minds. I want an answer by ten A.M. Mr. Blackarc will accompany you back to Three Acres."

"No way," I said. "No way do I want this traitor anywhere near me."

Uncle Larry tried to speak up. "Josh . . ."

"This guy was just a spy. All this time I thought he was the coolest guy in the world, teaching me all that stuff, and all the time he was just trying to get us."

Falco said, "About the deal . . ."

"No deal," I said, getting mad, really mad. "Grizzle left me the money, he left me everything. I've still got people on my side, and we're gonna prove it. You can keep Blackarc. You guys deserve each other."

"You're taking this very personally," said Falco. "These are strictly business decisions."

"Everything's personal," I said. I was still holding the little globe of the earth. I let it drop; it broke into three pieces when it hit the floor.

"You're going to be sorry you ever met me," said Falco as Uncle Larry and I left the office.

I said, "Too late, I'm *already* sorry."

Crazy

This is the embarrassing part of my story. This is the part about how I lost my mind.

Blackarc taught me what the word betrayal meant—as in "stab me in the back." Now I was going to teach myself the true meaning of the word greed.

"Greed: acquisitive or selfish desire beyond reason."

The key words there are "beyond reason."

When I went on my spending spree, nothing was beyond reason. What follows are only the highlights of my adventures in the weeks after Blackarc left Three Acres.

My freak-out started, as such freak-outs often do, very casually. I was feeling very bummed out about being messed over so badly by Blackarc, so I was spending most of my time in the video room of the mansion. This was one of the oddest places at Three Acres, considering how much of an intellectual Grizzle Welsch had been. The room had nothing in it but video games and big screen TVs, dozens of them. And not home games,

102

either—the arcade versions. But they didn't take money. You could just press START and dive right in.

I was living in that room after school, eating there, playing *Rocket Monsters* and *Dragonslayer* over and over again, with a bunch of guys around. In their constant effort to cheer me up, they kept bothering me. Half the time after Blackarc left I felt like a quarterback, surrounded by all those guys who huddled up around me whenever I made a move.

"I know," said one. "Why don't you do something?"

"You've got the weekend coming up," said another.

"Good idea," I said. "Norman?"

"Yeah?"

"Call the school tomorrow and tell them I'll be late coming in."

Norman hesitated. "How late?"

"Oh . . . How about February?"

Norman took a deep breath. "Josh, you can't do that."

"I can do anything I want. I'm the richest kid in the world."

"Yes, but there are still laws. You have to go to school."

"Oh, yeah? Guess what, Normie?"

"What?"

"You're fired. You're history. You're out of here."

"What?"

I looked him right in the eye. "I may have to

go to school, but I don't have to put up with you telling me I have to. 'Bye."

Norman's back stiffened. "As you wish," he said. He left the room.

For a second I felt bad, just for a second. It was like I was the king, ordering "Off with his head!" Which I guess in a way I was. Yeah, I was the king. That's the way I started acting, too. Whenever somebody told me I couldn't, or shouldn't, do something, I just said, "Fine, you're fired," and he was gone. Most of the time I'd hire him right back the next day, but not always. Not always.

Word got back to Grizzle (or into Grizzle, since somebody obviously typed on a keyboard, ratting on me) and he wasn't pleased. "Josh," he said from the screen in my room. "You're losing sight of what you should be doing."

"No I'm not."

"I'm told you spend all your time playing video games. A great waste of time. Foolish."

"Waste of time? If it's so foolish, why do you have all the games in your house?"

"Because some people do enjoy those things, and I never felt that everybody had to agree with me."

Ouch.

"The video game is an oddity in this world," Grizzle continued. "We all want peace in our real lives, yet so many find amusement in mindless armies battling on dark computer screens."

"Right, right," I said. "Are you mad because I've fired all your buddies?"

Grizzle hesitated, then finished by saying, "Only

you can question your own judgement. Just be sure of what you do."

I nodded, because he was right.

I was king.

The only problem was, it was lonely at the top.

Oh, I had plenty of people around me, but no friends. The guys from school all wanted to help me buy things, but we never just played ball anymore, or goofed around or anything. Even Miss Lisa didn't want anything much to do with me.

Another funny thing was, all the while we never heard a peep out of Falco. I was buying things—clothes, video games, TVs, pizzas—spending Grizzle's money like it was going out of style, and Falco never raised a finger to stop me. He just quietly kept about his business—bad business, it turned out.

Uncle Larry was loving it. He was working very hard at not working. I didn't do my homework for six weeks, and Uncle Larry didn't get out of the pool for three days straight. He just sat around eating shrimp and lobster and crab and other disgusting things while he worked on his tan.

Which was fine. That's what he was paid for.

Me, I was paying myself to do absolutely everything in my power to make everybody I knew hate me.

"This isn't what Grizzle meant the money to be used for," said my lawyer Andy. She wanted to get serious with me. Apparently she was one of the few people who were not ready to stand and watch as I became a rich-waste-of-life-dweeb.

I was floating around in the pool on a rubber mat. Just like Uncle Larry, but I wasn't quite ready to eat crab or lobster. Memo to myself number six-oh-four: Never eat anything that looks like a radioactive spider.

"Come on, Andy, what's annoying you now?" I asked. I was used to this kind of talk, but still didn't like hearing it.

"What's annoying me is the way you guys are living."

That got my attention. "What's wrong with the way I'm living?"

"It's sick. You and your uncle have become greedheads."

"Have not."

"Have so."

I thought for a second about just firing her, telling her to pack up and walk, but then I decided against it. I just said, "Look, you get what you want, don't you? What's the big deal?"

"Three Acres is supposed to be more than just fun. It's a creative foundation."

"Is that what it is? All this time I thought it was my house."

Andy huffed a bit. She said, "Scientists work here on disease cures. Artistic people paint, sculpt, write plays, music. People here teach each other things, and learn."

"So?"

"So you're stopping them from doing that. All you want to do is have fun."

"What is the matter with fun?" I asked, falling off of the mat and swimming to the side of the pool. I looked up at her, wiping dripping water from my face.

"There's more to life than fun," she said. "There's responsibility, for one thing. Not everybody can live the way you do."

"So? I was poor once."

"Yes." She thought about that a long, long moment. "I probably would have liked you better when you were poor."

She walked away then, but Miss Lisa came to see me the next day, and she was just as annoyed with me.

"Mellow out," I said.

"You're doing all of this just because of Blackarc, aren't you?"

"Forget about Blackarc."

"What's wrong with you, Josh?"

"Nothing's wrong with me."

"You're flunking everything at school."

"So?"

"So you might get set back a year."

"People as rich as me don't get set back a year."

"You keep firing people."

"Yeah. And I keep hiring them back."

"That doesn't make it right."

"Who ever said it had to be right?"

Miss Lisa shook her head in total disgust. "What does Grizzle have to say about all of this?"

"Not much."

"You know what I mean."

"Yeah," I said. "I just don't care to hear what you mean."

Miss Lisa gave out this really big sigh. "You're not even having fun anymore, Josh."

That annoyed me. "Yes, I am. Fun is my middle name. No, fun is my *first* name. I am Mister Fun."

"Josh, come on. Nobody can eat chocolate for every meal."

"No. Sometimes I have ice cream."

They were right, though. My mind was starting to wander. I was thinking a lot about Carlos, and the old school, the good times we had. I was even thinking about Uncle Larry, the way he'd been before the money came. He'd usually ignored me then, but not all the time, not like now.

Most of all I wondered what Blackarc was up to.

Blackarc. That geek. I trusted him and he did this to me. Well, we were going to show him, but good. We were going to live high and live big, and if he and Falco wanted to sneak around and plot, so be it. I got out of the pool, took a shower, got dressed, and went up to my room.

Little did I know that I was coming face to face with a capital letter M—for *M*oment of Truth. Memo to myself number nine: When your life takes a sudden turn, it's probably because somebody else has just grabbed the steering wheel.

When I went into the elevator to go upstairs it didn't say anything to me. At first I thought it was broken. "I want to go to my room," I said. "I'm a little tired."

"Whatever," answered the elevator, closing its

doors. Slowly. It sounded even more sarcastic than usual, if that was possible.

"What the heck is with you?" I asked.

"Me? Nothing. I'm just a stupid old elevator, just a piece of talking machinery. What could be wrong with me?"

I shrugged.

Then the elevator stopped between floors and said, "Okay, I'll tell you what's wrong with me, mister richest kid in the world. Maybe I just don't like your attitude. Maybe I just don't like the way you've been acting."

"Fine, who asked you?"

"What?" The elevator was bouncing up and down between floors now, it was so aggravated. I just held onto the handrail and bounced along with it. The elevator kept yelling at me: "You can't treat people the way you have! You can't use people like that!"

Sheesh! Even the elevator was out to get me now! "What do you care how I treat people? You're just an elevator!"

"Oh, yeah, insult me. Well, I may just be an elevator, but I've got friends. Have you counted *your* friends lately? Huh?"

I thought a second. "The stairs are my friend! How about if I just walk from now on? Huh?"

"Oh, that's *real* good. Your best friend in the world is a set of talking stairs!"

The elevator doors opened then, before I could think of an answer. We were at the penthouse level and I got off. I had to sigh. This was totally stupid. What the heck had happened to my brain?

Depressed, I went into my room.

The voice-controlled computer was over on the desk and I started to say something, but stopped. I hadn't actually talked to Grizzle in weeks, and now I felt bad. It was almost as if I were ungrateful or something. Finally I cleared my throat and said . . . "Uh, Grizzle? You there?"

Pip! In an instant the image popped on, and Grizzle was smiling on the TV set. "Well, hello. It's been awhile."

"Yeah."

"I only mention it because I am not only a computer, I am also the biggest clock in the house. Need to know what time it is?"

"No."

"What's up?"

I swallowed, cleared my throat some, then told him the story of the last few weeks, about Blackarc's turning out to be a bad guy, and about my spending spree. "I don't know what happened," I said finally. "I think I've gone crazy."

Grizzle looked thoughtful a moment. "Maybe. But do you feel crazy now?"

"No," I said, taking off the rings and watches and gold chains I was wearing. "I just feel stupid. And depressed."

Grizzle nodded. "Well. You've learned, and you've learned well."

"Huh?"

"The easiest way to break someone of eating candy is to let him eat all the candy he wants for a while. Do you want any more candy?"

110

"You mean do I want to go crazy again? No, thanks. I just want things to be back to normal."

"Well . . . we'll see," said Grizzle. "The thing is, I wanted—and still want—you to be the one to take care of things now that I'm gone. But as good a kid as you were—are—I knew that you'd need a little education."

"You mean like school?"

"Sort of like school, yes. But our own sort of private school of hard knocks. I think you're ready to graduate. You've learned about greed. And the value of friends. And about betrayal."

That perked my ears. "Say what?"

Grizzle was grinning. "Blackarc isn't really a bad guy, Josh. Everything he did was on my orders, to help you think on your feet, make your own decisions. I want him to be there by your side to help, but in the end you'll be the one in charge and that takes some . . . independence."

I hardly heard most of that, I was still caught up in the big news. "You mean Blackarc isn't really working for Falco?"

Grizzle laughed. "Of course not. That's just a game being played to keep Falco overconfident while we finish up the transfer of power to you."

"Blackarc's on our side?"

"Yes. He always has been."

"And the will and stuff?"

Grizzle-the-computer thought a moment and made a big decision. "It's time to place it in your hands. You have a big court date in a week or so, so I'll tell you now. The documents you need to prove your claim to the money are—"

Beep. Beep! BEEP!
Everything went black.
Why?
That was when all the lights, the power, and all the computers in the house died.

The Shaft

The world was falling apart.

All the lights were out and the computers had died, but a few seconds later alarm bells started ringing and the computer came back on. Sort of.

It wasn't Grizzle now, just some words:

SYSTEMS FAILURE IN PROGRESS.

"Oh, no . . ."

EMERGENCY, said the computer. CODE KEY ACCESS AT SUBBASEMENT ONLY. RESET EMERGENCY.

What that all meant, I had no idea, but it didn't take a smart guy to know it couldn't be good.

I went out into the hallway. It was dark, but I saw the beam of a flashlight bouncing towards me. It was Norman and Feldman, and they were in a panic. "Are you all right?" Norman asked, reaching out and grabbing me by the shoulder.

It hit me right then that this *was* Norman, the one guy I'd fired who wouldn't come back when I asked him to. "Norman! You're back!"

"Yes, but—"

"I'm glad to see you, man, it's good to see you."

"Yes, I—"

"Really, man, really. I'm sorry. I've been really stupid lately. I know that. I just want you guys to know I've come to my senses and I'm going to try to be a normal person. No more adventures."

Even by the dim light of the flashlight I could see they didn't look happy.

"What's wrong? I just said I was sorry."

Feldman shook his head. "We've got big problems, Josh."

"What?"

They explained it to me. The whole house was computer controlled—all the lights, doors, locks, everything.

"Yeah, I know. So we have to wait."

"We can't wait. This is Falco's doing. Andy just called to say he was on his way over, they want the will *now,* or else they've got a court order to throw you and your uncle out and take over everything. Now something is destroying the computer, that's why this is happening."

"I don't understand. What am I supposed to do?" They were looking to me for answers—and I knew if I was the answer man, we were all in trouble.

Then I remembered the computer key. The card around my neck.

I didn't get the answer I wanted, though. The screen in Grizzle's study said:

ACCESS DENIED
EMERGENCY STAT
STATION ONE ACCESS ONLY

114

Station one? Station one was the machine in the subbasement, the one I talked to sometimes.

Wonderful. And the elevator wasn't working. The computer blowout had shut it all down.

"What am I supposed to do?"

Norman knew. He said, "You've got to go down."

"Go down?"

"Climb down."

"Me?"

"You have the code key, you climb."

He had me there.

So they outfitted me with a flashlight and a rope, and got me set up for a little mountain climbing in the elevator shaft.

"You gotta climb fast," said Feldman.

"I know," I said. "We're all going nuts being locked in here."

"No, no," he said. *"We're* all right; *you* gotta climb down fast."

"Why?"

"Security system. Supposed to keep out robbers, bad men. *Especially* keep them out of basements."

"What are you trying to say, Feldman?"

"You don't know about lasers?"

"What lasers? What are you talking about?"

"Automatic defense system," he said. "In the elevator shaft, it'll slow you down some. The system goes on when the alarms do, when the computer dies."

"Hold it a second," I said, feeling a little stupid standing there with a rope around my waist and the big flashlight in my hand. "Are you trying to tell me that elevator shaft is full of killer laser beams? Like out of some science fiction movie?"

"No, no, not full. There's only, er, seven, I think."

"Seven killer laser beams?"

"Eight, really, but we're lucky. One of them is down for repairs."

"Oh. So *we're* lucky."

"Yeah."

"So why don't *I* feel lucky?"

Feldman shrugged.

They explained what I was going to have to do. The elevator had a trap door on the ceiling, which they were prying open. First I had to climb up on top of the elevator, then squeeze my way down beside it, then lower myself by rope down to the bottom of the shaft—all while keeping an eye out for killer laser beams which would be trying to turn me into a crispy critter.

I had even bigger worries right then, though. The shaft was pretty deep. "You sure this is enough rope to make it all the way down?"

"No." Feldman looked at Norman. They both shrugged.

"Terrific."

"You asked."

"Yeah, but doesn't anybody around here ever just *lie* about anything? It's okay, you know. You could just say sure, sure, Josh. Plenty of rope. Don't worry about a thing."

"What good would that do?"

"Just get me up on top of this elevator."

116

They did. It was spooky, crawling around up there—even more so because on most days the elevator talked. Now it was a lot like having some cold, dead, steel dinosaur beneath my feet.

Oh, well. At least it was dark. I could only see as far as my flashlight beam, and that was probably for the best.

"Josh!" Feldman was yelling up at me, just before I crawled down over the side and into the pit.

"Yeah, what?"

"If you get killed, can I have your baseball cards?"

"Funny, guy, real—"

I slipped.

"Hey!" I yelled, feeling my balance go. As easy as you please, I slid right over the side of that elevator and started to drop like a brick. But I managed to grab hold of the top of the car with one hand and hold on for dear life.

"You okay?"

"No!"

"The rope's snug tight. Start on down."

I looked below me. Good thing the flashlight was chained to my belt. Not that it mattered: there was nothing but darkness below me. I pulled it back up and started to lower myself down.

Quiet.

All the alarms had stopped ringing. It was just me in the black elevator shaft, crawling down as slowly and steadily as I could, hoping the rope would be long enough, trying not to bounce off the wall too much.

Oh, well, I thought again. At least I don't have to see—

Ziiiing! Zeep!

I froze.

Something bright and yellow had just flashed by my left ear, setting my hair on end. I tried to figure out what it was. It was like a ray gun on *Star Trek* or something, was like a—

I let myself drop. And not a second too soon, because an orange zing zapped right where I'd been the second before, singeing the wall a bit. I could hear the sizzle and smell the electric burning smell.

Memo to myself, casual thought number seven-twenty-one: Now I know what it's like to be on the wrong end of a video game.

Come on, come on. How much farther could it be?

Something bumped my foot, the right one, and I saw the light and heard the wall sizzling again. Missed me by quarter of an inch, maybe. Time to drop some more, and fast.

They said there were seven lasers. How many was that so far? It might help if I could keep track. Yellow, orange, burning sneaker, and—

"Ahhhh!" I was screaming, because *my foot was on fire!* A laser cut the rope in half then, and I fell. But believe it or not, that was good, because even though my foot was burning it beat being zapped by the two lasers which had fired—both at the same time—at the exact spot where I'd

118

been one second before. Not to mention the one that had zipped by below me just before I fell.

How far to fall? That was all I wondered before I hit bottom. If it was still ten or twenty feet, I didn't figure I'd bounce.

Bam! No bounce required, because I was definitely on the bottom and my back hurt. I tried to raise the flashlight to look around, but a laser nailed it. The light flickered and the plastic heated up and started to melt before I got smart enough to drop the stupid thing.

I fell to my knees and tensed, expecting to get fried. But it was only a few feet, thank goodness, to the subbasement doors. I pulled and pried at them in the dark, happy to see that the emergency lights inside were working. Before I could get turned into a french fry, I scrambled inside and squeezed the doors closed behind me. Just in time, too, because I could hear the zing of the last laser hitting the closing elevator doors.

Safe! Or sort of, anyway. I fumbled with the code key and got the computer working. Grizzle's face appeared on the screen, but it was different.

"Dover Beach," he said. "By Matthew Arnold."

"What's wrong?" I asked. "Grizzle, what's going on?"

He jerked a bit and spoke to me. "Someone has broken into my computer system. A hacker, a computer terrorist, somebody or someone. A new program was stuck in, and it is destroying me."

I was in a panic. "What do I do? How can I stop it?"

Grizzle shook his head, but then I saw he was

stuck shaking his head; that's all the image on screen could do right now. "Nothing. There's nothing to be done. I've tried blocking access to some of my memory systems, but Falco's man has done a good job."

"Falco? That slime. There's got to be something we can do."

"No. I tried to print up the instructions for you, but none of my print systems are working. I—"

His face jerked again; he was quoting something, a poem: " 'The sea is calm tonight . . .' "

"Sea? Grizzle, come back!"

He did. "I'm sorry, Josh. I'm breaking down. I can't seem to confirm any of my information."

"Come *on!*"

"This thing is some sort of computer virus. It's unraveling me from top to bottom. It's . . . killing me."

"No way," I said. "*Do* something."

"I'm going now. I can feel it. There's less and less to me. All my money couldn't keep me around." His voice was slowing down, growing fainter.

"Grizzle!"

"My mind is going, Josh. I can feel it. I can . . . feel it."

I looked around fast, banging on the equipment, but I didn't know what to do. "No, come on, Grizzle, you can't do this to me now, not now, not with Falco on his way over here with the cops. Grizzle, come on! Help me! Where's the will? Where's the proof?"

His image froze a second, then moved again,

speaking slowly. " 'And ...'" he said, obviously quoting something again. " 'We are here ... as on a darkling plain.' "

"Grizzle ..."

" 'Swept with confused alarms of struggle and flight ...' "

"Grizzle, come on, don't do this to me."

" 'Swept,' " he repeated. " 'Swept, swept, swept ...' "

"Grizzle!"

" 'Where ignorant armies clash by night.' "

"I need to ..."

I stopped talking. The screen—all the screens— were covered with white snow. The power was back on for some reason, but Grizzle Welsch was gone forever.

Lyle

"Come on, rich boy," Lyle Walker was yelling, dragging me on our way to the midst of the gravel lot. "Come on and get what's coming to you."

Lyle was the legend.

Lyle was the King of the Ninth Grade.

I was home again, back in plain old clothes, back in the vacant lot and about to get thrashed like always and, like always, none too thrilled about it.

Memo to myself, number forty-six: If you ever have a chance to be a multi-billionaire, don't blow it. Too many bad side effects when you become poor again.

I became poor just as quickly as I'd become rich; Falco came to Three Acres personally to see Uncle Larry and me out. They came down on us pretty hard when we couldn't come up with the will or other documents to prove Grizzle meant to leave me all the money.

How they did it I didn't know. Grizzle was gone, there was no way to ask him. Things had happened to him so fast he . . .

There I went again. He? *It*. Grizzle was just a computer, just a bunch of microchips and stuff. There wasn't any sense getting all upset about it. I used to have a tape recorder and I didn't go all mushy when *it* broke, did I?

No. But then again, my tape recorder didn't die, break, whatever by quoting a weird poem to me. 'Darkling plain?' 'Ignorant armies?' What was that all supposed to mean?

Nothing, I told myself. The computer broke, that was all.

Falco and the other executives came out after the computer broke, and they brought some mean looking U.S. marshals and some orders from a judge telling us we had to leave. They were right on top of things, and they moved very fast.

"You'll take nothing with you, either," Falco said. "Just the clothes you had on when you got here."

"What about our other stuff?" asked Uncle Larry. "Our trailer, the furniture?"

"It's being returned," said Falco, very smugly. "We've sent down to the city dump to recover it all."

"Doesn't bother me," I said. "I'd rather have our stuff out of the dump than have anything you'd want to give us."

Falco just smiled. Then he said, "You're both very fortunate we don't prosecute for fraud."

"Hah!" I said. "Who are you kidding? You know you set us up. You programmed the computer to self-destruct before it could tell us where the will and stuff is. You know you're lying. You know what you're doing is wrong."

"I didn't do anything."

"You killed Grizzle."

Falco seemed very sure of himself. "I'm doing what's best for the corporation."

"What about the people?"

"People?"

"The people here at Three Acres. The foundation, the Associates."

"Oh, yes. The people. I'll be making the announcement in the Great Hall this afternoon. As for the rest of the goof-offs and freeloaders here, they have thirty days. Then I'm having the place bulldozed down."

"Why?"

"We're putting in a shopping mall. Three Acres Shopping Complex." Falco used my own words against me: "You know, 'One more mall pretzel place.'"

"Come on, Falco," I said. "I know you don't like me or Uncle Larry, but you can't do this to the Three Acres people. What about the projects? The experiments? The art and stuff? This place is great."

"This place is history," he said.

And that was that.

I said goodbye to the staff people, to Andy the lawyer, to Norman, and Feldman, and even to the elevator and stairs, although they couldn't talk anymore. I would have said goodbye to Miss Lisa too, but she was nowhere around when I got ready to leave.

Probably for the best, I thought.

All that was left was to fly us back home, back into our old lives (well, sort of. Uncle Larry's old boss was still mad from when Uncle Larry had told him to "take his job and shove it," so we were probably going to have a few problems in the food department.).

I felt almost at rock bottom, but when I sat down beside Mike the pilot I cheered up some. My last flight; I might as well enjoy it. After we took off, I started to take the control stick but he stopped me.

"Sorry, kid. Mr. Falco's orders. You're not supposed to touch any of the controls." And, he just stared straight ahead, like he couldn't even see me.

I watched out the window as the helicopter started to rise. I thought I saw Miss Lisa peeking out of a window, watching it lift off, but I wasn't sure.

So, it finally, finally hit me. I was poor.

Not that I cared about the money. (Okay, so I did care about the money, but cash isn't everything, is it? Is it?)

No, health was much more important than cash, and I was about to lose mine as Lyle got ready to pound me right into the middle of next week.

He'd wanted to ever since I first showed up back at school. That was embarrassing enough, but Lyle and his buddies did their best to make me even more miserable. Homeroom was the first place where I had to show my face and face the truth: I was just another kid again.

Just another small kid.

My homeroom teacher Ms. Wangowski smiled sadly; I guess she felt sorry for me, or else she was just thinking how she might feel if she was in the same situation. "Welcome back, Josh."

I nodded, but didn't say anything.

All things considered, at least the people who had been my friends before weren't as vicious as they might have been. They didn't exactly rush over with pats on the back to welcome me back, but at least they were saying hi, nodding hello, that kind of thing.

My school locker had a lock on it again.

Oh, well.

I was humiliated, but I was at least smart enough to know that some of the humiliation was my own fault. If I hadn't made such a big deal out of being rich, then being poor again wouldn't have been such a problem.

Justice was due, and justice was being served by Lyle.

Grabbing me, Lyle pulled at my windbreaker. "How does it feel to be poor again?" he asked. "How does it feel to be the nobody you really are?"

I thought a whole two seconds. "It sucks," I said.

Lyle glared. "When I get through with you, you're gonna have to ask for directions just to find your head."

Oops.

Definitely oops.

I wondered what Blackarc would do in a situation like this?

What would Grizzle do?

Lyle shoved me down again; I cut the back of my left hand as I went down. I looked up and saw them all then, all the kids who always came to these stupid fights to watch. A week ago they'd all wanted to be my buddy. Now I was just another spectator sport.

Lyle tried to kick me, but I rolled out of the way. Instead of getting zonked I just got dirtier. It was only going to be worse on me, though, because Lyle was near a junk pile now and he pulled out a board, a long hunk of wood.

He cannot be serious, I thought.

Memo to myself number twenty-two: When the bullies start grabbing sticks to hit you over the head with, it's time for a whole new bunch of bullies.

I was about to get stomped, and there wasn't anything I could do about it. Or . . . was there?

Lyle didn't have the only piece of wood from the lot. I grabbed a broken broom handle, and as I jerked it up into my hands I went from desperate . . . to calm.

Yeah. Oh, yeah.

I even smiled.

Yeah. I had to laugh. Yeah.

Lyle was doomed.

He was doomed, and he didn't even know it yet.

Blackarc may have not been there to help me,

but before my life fell apart he had taught me something: how to fence a little. A little bit more than Lyle, anyway, because Lyle swung with the hunk of wood he was carrying and I didn't even flinch. I just casually stepped to the left with the move Blackarc had taught me that first day, and deflected Lyle's blow with my broom handle.

It all happened so fast Lyle didn't even have a chance to realize it. He swung again, and this time I stood my ground and brought my broom handle up in the classic fencing position. I met his blow, blocked his weapon, and then pushed hard to the left, knocking it clean out of his hands.

"En garde," I said. I couldn't help myself.

Lyle didn't quit. He backed off, ran over, and picked up his weapon again. He was a little nervous now, but that just made him more dangerous, because he wasn't going to make the same sort of stupid mistake twice.

No, now all Lyle wanted to do was knock my head off.

Wonderful. What the heck was I doing?

We fought for a while, blocking each other's blows, but he was stronger than I was, and I was backing up all the while. Pretty soon, though, I'd backed right up to one of the junk piles. Now I was back in my pirate movie, climbing up and down the sloping decks of the ship.

Yeah. I took a quick look, and although there was no rope to swing from, I jumped, down about three and a half feet. I hit the ground just right, bending my knees the way Blackarc had taught me. Lyle followed, but he didn't land so well. He didn't fall, but I could tell he'd hurt one of his legs doing it.

We sword fought with our wooden swords awhile as the crowd of kids gave us room. Now we were working our way towards a dead car, the broken hulk of a rusty old Ford which had been in the vacant lot for as long as I could remember. I jumped up on the hood now, fighting and climbing higher as Lyle took swipes at my feet. I bounced my way right up to the car roof now, and Lyle went absolutely out of his mind.

"Get down from there, you chicken!"

"What's the matter, Lyle? Having brain bubbles?"

"Arrrgh!"

I jumped off the other side of the car and took off, with Lyle in hot pursuit. When I found a good spot, I stopped and spun around, fighting all out now, going for broke.

Whack! Whack-whack!

"I have you now!" I yelled, and Lyle's eyes went wide because he knew it, too. One more blow and his board flew out of his hands. But I didn't let up. I kept coming. Within seconds, my broom handle was pressed up against his chin.

(Okay, it would have been a better story if it was a sword but hey, all I had was a broom handle.)

"What say you all?" I asked the crowd of kids. "Shall I whack him upside the head?"

"Yeah!" They yelled. "Do it!"

Lyle cringed. Of everybody there, he was obviously the one most sure he deserved it.

I'd love to say I whacked him. I'd love to say I just beat the heck out of him with that stick, but . . . I didn't. What I did do was back off and toss the broom handle away, because I realized how stupid we must look. We were just like Grizzle's silly poem, we were two one-man ignorant armies fighting it out—and for what? For nothing. This wasn't important. We might as well have been playing video games or something and—

Oh, my gosh.

The kids around me were applauding and cheering and so was I then, inside, because I'd just realized what the poem meant. Grizzle hadn't been crazy in the end. He'd been smart, and the poem was a code, and I was going to be rich again—I knew it—and after Lyle, the one guy I really wanted to smack with a broomstick was Kurt Falco, C.E.O. of Grizzco International. And I was going to get my chance. . . .

Me and My Buddy Falco

When Uncle Larry and I showed up back at Three Acres they were not exactly happy to see us. I could have saved Three Acres and I blew it. Very unforgiving bunch.

I passed Miss Lisa in the Great Hall and she looked totally shocked. "Josh! What are you doing here?"

Pointing a finger I said, "Just stay out of my way." I kept walking.

"What?" She followed after us.

"Trust me." I kept walking.

She caught up and fell into step with me. "What are you guys doing? Three Acres is over, everybody's packing."

"Tell everybody to stop packing," I said.

"What?"

"You heard me. I know where the will is. I can prove my claim, and I'm going to get Falco."

Her eyes were wide and she stopped in her tracks. "Really?"

"Really," I said. I stopped walking and said, "Tell everybody to stop packing and get your mom. I'm going to need my lawyer."

"*Your* lawyer?" Miss Lisa frowned.

I know she was thinking about when I was nuts so I said, "Yeah, but it's okay. This time I'm going to do everything right."

Miss Lisa was leaving just as Norman found us climbing the steps. "You're not supposed to be here."

"Tell me about it," said a very nervous Uncle Larry. He kept looking back over his shoulder.

"Mr. Falco gave orders to call the police."

I frowned. "You're not going to do that, are you Norman?"

He looked nervous. "It's not up to me. Somebody already called, I think."

"Great. How long will it take them to get here?"

He shrugged. "I don't know. Five, ten, maybe fifteen minutes."

"That'll have to be enough," I said, tearing off through the house.

Norman followed. "Where are you going? What are you doing?"

"The poem!" I said, clapping my hands together. "Grizzle's last words! I thought he was crazy, the computer goofing up, but he was sending me a code, trying to tell me where the will and stuff were hidden."

"Really?" This excited him. "Where?"

"The arcade," I said. "The video game room. 'Where ignorant armies clash by night.' See, the guys fighting on the computer games aren't real, they don't know anything. They're ignorant. Somewhere in the arcade room the will's hidden. I know it!"

Norman and Uncle Larry both looked amazed that I had thought all that out myself. Norman said, "The cops are on the way. We won't have time to find it."

"We can try, can't we?"

"Sure, but—"

"No but. Look."

We did. I could try to make the scene exciting, but it's enough to say we found the stuff inside the back of one of the big video games. Andy showed up, looking kind of aggravated, but when she read what I had found her eyes started to glow.

"Is it enough to make Falco crazy?" I asked.

"Josh," she said. "This is enough to make Falco double crazy . . ."

Both doors to the boardroom flew open wide; one of them banged off a wall. The directors, a bunch of guys just like Falco, stopped in mid-discussion, and a few of them stood up. We were followed in by a bunch of nervous secretaries and others. I marched right up to a very, very surprised Mr. Falco.

I was smiling.

"Wha . . . what is going on here?" He didn't bother to wait for an answer. Instead he reached

133

down and pushed a button. "Security! Security to the conference room!"

"It's okay," I said. "I brought security guards with me."

"What?"

Three guards came in, led by my bodyguard, Feldman.

I looked over at Andy. "Tell him."

First Andy pushed a bunch of papers at Falco, saying, "What you see here are copies of documents already filed in court. A living trust, it seems, establishing Josh Ellis as co-trustee of the estate, with full rights of survivorship when Mr. Welsch expired."

Falco looked confused, and this time *I* translated for Andy: "It's mine, Falco, it's all mine. It always has been."

"What?"

"I own seventy-five percent of the stock in this company. *I'm* your boss."

He knew it was true, and he tried to tap dance his way out of trouble. "Well, if this is true that does change things entirely, of course."

"Sure does, Falco. You're fired."

"I beg your pardon?"

"Did I stutter? Clean out your desk, beat it, adios, get lost."

"What?"

Andy handed him some more papers and said, "You have thirty minutes to clean your personal items out of your office and be off company property. After that you could be arrested for trespassing."

Falco slammed his fists down. "This is outrageous."

"Tell it to the people at the unemployment office."

"You can't do this!"

"No? Feldman, explain it all to Mr. Falco, will you?"

My bodyguard stepped up, grabbed Falco by the arm, and took him out of the conference room. I pointed at Falco's rude assistants and said, "They go, too."

"Yes, sir."

I looked at the rest of the board of directors. "There are going to be a lot of changes around here," I said.

They waited.

"First off," I said, settling into Falco's desk, "from now on we can't have these meetings on school days . . ."

Actually, to be honest, after I fired Falco I almost walked away from all the money. Seriously. I figured, who needed all the aggravation? Besides, I'd already had my big spending spree. I was sort of burned out.

Still, I did come to my senses.

"Okay," I said. "I'll take the money on three conditions."

"Oh, thank God," said Uncle Larry.

Blackarc looked amused. He was back with us now, still as mysterious as ever. "What are your conditions?"

"First of all, I make my own decisions. I really

135

hated it when you guys kept talking over and around me like I wasn't even in the room."

Blackarc nodded, pleased. "Agreed."

"Secondly, Three Acres goes on, just like before."

"Of course."

"Third, find me something exciting to do with my life. Things are way too boring around here . . ."

Celebrating 40 Years of Cleary Kids!

CAMELOT presents
CLEARY FAVORITES!

- ☐ **HENRY HUGGINS**
  70912-0 ($3.50 US/$4.25 Can)

- ☐ **HENRY AND BEEZUS**
  70914-7 ($3.50 US/$4.25 Can)

- ☐ **HENRY AND THE CLUBHOUSE**
  70915-5 ($3.50 US/$4.25 Can)

- ☐ **ELLEN TEBBITS**
  70913-9 ($3.50 US/$4.25 Can)

- ☐ **HENRY AND RIBSY**
  70917-1 ($3.50 US/$4.25 Can)

- ☐ **BEEZUS AND RAMONA**
  70918-X ($3.50 US/$4.25 Can)

- ☐ **RAMONA AND HER FATHER**
  70916-3 ($3.50 US/$4.25 Can)

- ☐ **MITCH AND AMY**
  70925-2 ($3.50 US/$4.25 Can)

- ☐ **RUNAWAY RALPH**
  70953-8 ($3.50 US/$4.25 Can)

- ☐ **HENRY AND THE PAPER ROUTE**
  70921-X ($3.50 US/$4.25 Can)

- ☐ **RAMONA AND HER MOTHER**
  70952-X ($3.50 US/$4.25 Can)

- ☐ **OTIS SPOFFORD**
  70919-8 ($3.50 US/$4.25 Can)

- ☐ **THE MOUSE AND THE MOTORCYCLE**
  70924-4 ($3.50 US/$4.25 Can)

- ☐ **SOCKS**
  70926-0 ($3.50 US/$4.25 Can)

- ☐ **EMILY'S RUNAWAY IMAGINATION**
  70923-6 ($3.50 US/$4.25 Can)

- ☐ **MUGGIE MAGGIE**
  71087-0 ($3.50 US/$4.25 Can)